I Heard You Scream

EMERALD
O'BRIEN

For Meghan,
who guides me through the trees
until I see the forest.

1

It's difficult to see things coming in the eye of a storm.

A raven sits on a wire, glaring at me. The light beside it glows green with the gray sky behind it. Cam drives forward through the intersection, and I close my eyes. I fight to keep saliva from pooling in my mouth by clenching my stomach muscles repetitively, almost involuntarily. My heart races, pounding in my ears as I grip the seatbelt across my chest, pulling it away to take full, purposeful breaths.

Breathing is the key to most things in life.

Cam was right to suggest the Xanax before we left, despite the fuss I put up about it. Begrudgingly, I took it. Somehow, agreeing to take the little white coffin-shaped pill felt like a dead giveaway; Cam might uncover that there's more to this day—this memorial—than anyone could ever know. I wouldn't risk him catching a glimpse of fear in my eyes.

His hand glides over the polyester wrap of my dress against my thigh, up my lap, and into my hand, lacing his fingers in mine. He twists at the diamond ring he placed on my index finger a few months ago in a nervous, fidgeting manner. I often do the same. It's a mindless motion that eats at me with each twist. In mere seconds, he's ratcheted my anxiety levels through the roof.

I don't want him touching me. I don't want to be here.

I squeeze both my hands over his to make him stop without having to speak. The stillness prevents my skin from crawling with frustration for long enough to take another deep breath.

He's just trying to offer support. Don't push him away like you always do—not today.

I squeeze his hand and his stops moving. Much better.

The relief doesn't last long.

"Did Jordan contact you at all yet?" Cam's smooth, deep voice interrupts the silence as he switches lanes with one hand.

I need to breathe. Just keep breathing.

"Chels?"

He stares at me, his dapper suit hugging him in a perfect fit against his solid frame, waiting for a response.

"No." Attitude permeates the word as I turn my whole body away from him toward the window. I expect to see that raven still watching me, but the sky only offers mottled clouds.

Cam mutters something, but I don't catch it. I inhale deeply through my nose as my muscles tense, and exhale through my lips. Don't let him bait you. Just keep breathing. I can still taste the remnants of Xanax on my tongue. It'll kick in soon. It always does.

"I just don't understand why he wouldn't check in

today." His body shifts toward me in my peripheral. "Of *all days*."

My clenched jaw doesn't stop me from speaking. "This isn't a surprise. That's how my brother is, and you wouldn't know because you've never met him."

"I know if my brother or sister had been through even a fraction of what you have, I'd have been there for them. That's what siblings do, Chels, and I'm sorry yours hasn't been there for you."

I can't explain it to him any better than I have before, and the fact that he insists on bringing him up now urges me to put it to bed for good. "He probably doesn't even know what day it is." As the lie leaves my lips, I peer over at Cam.

He raises his brows, staring at the road ahead. "The whole town knows what day it is. You shouldn't make excuses for him."

"I'm not. That's not why he hasn't called. You *know* why he hasn't."

"It just doesn't make any sense to me. Steven was his friend. *Fine*." He tosses his right hand in the air, shoving it back toward the steering wheel in the next motion. "I get how that complicates feelings but after what he did to—to all of you." He shakes his head as we veer left along the familiar curve in the road toward the water on the horizon. To the house where it all happened. "You're the only family Jordan has, and he's it for you, too. He should be here today. His loyalty is to *you*—not that monster."

Our mother passed after a battle with cancer when we were young, and our dad died of cirrhosis nearly a decade ago. I hated to be reminded that the only kin I had left hadn't spoken to me for almost five years.

I take a huge breath, my stomach heaving as I close my eyes and exhale through my lips. The pill must be kicking in because I can't hear my heartbeat anymore. It's muffled as the word *monster* echoes in my mind. I can't hear Cam's voice, the gentle hum of the car's engine, or even my own breathing.

But I see Steven behind my lids. His hands covered in blood, holding the knife.

"Jordan should be loyal to *you*. Y'know, maybe he'll surprise you. Maybe he'll be there—"

"Cam." I turn to him slowly and he stops, glancing at me and back to the road ahead. "Could you please drop it? I know how you feel. I have support. I have you. Kellan and Oz are coming, too. I'm okay. Today is going to be okay. It's just something we have to get through."

I told myself that on the first, second, third, and fourth anniversary of my friends' murders, and it was true. I made it through each of those days, and our secrets did, too.

"We'll get through it together, babe." He grabs my hand again, but I feel numb, unsure if it's the Xanax taking its course, or the stress-induced adrenaline running through me.

I give him a small smile. I've been alone for a long time, carrying the burden of truth. No matter how far I go from this town, or how much time passes, I'll never escape my past. I know that, now.

My eyes flutter open and closed as my body slumps back in the seat. Our car rolls to a stop at the end of a long line of cars parked in front of Lennox and Eliana's old house. The last place I saw my friends alive. Cam shifts into park. Across the street, a couple walks along the beach, unfazed by the dreariness of the day, unaware of the murders that took place close by.

"Would you be happy if he came?" His gentle tone and slow cadence keep me from shouting at him to stop. "Would you want to see him?"

His green eyes innocently search mine. He's just trying to be supportive. His intentions are good, but he doesn't understand. Jordan doesn't, either, and that's how I know he won't be there for me ever again.

"Jordan doesn't know how to deal with what happened." My gaze falls from him to the water along the horizon. "I don't, either, but I don't have the luxury of avoiding it like he does. He removed himself from all of it, Cam. He's not coming. The sooner you accept that, the less disappointment you'll feel."

"Your brother's best friend killed four of your closest friends." He shakes his head. "He almost killed you—would have if the cops hadn't shot him." He faces me, but I continue looking past him at the water, the choppy waves rolling slightly off-parallel to the shore. "If Jordan misses one more chance to show up for you in the way you need, I'll support your decision to let it be this way. No, you know what?" He pulls the keys from the ignition. "I'll make sure if he ever tries to come back, he knows the damage he's done, and he won't have another chance to hurt you."

I rub my temple, facing the frustration in his gaze as he grips the keys in his fist. That's a look I can take; I can handle that emotion today. I'd take that over the pity and judgement in the eyes soon to fall on me.

"Jordan never tried to understand what happened that night." I lick my lips and rest my hand on his fist. "He refused to believe his best friend was capable of—of what he did."

Beyond the white picket fence, the large wooden door of Lennox and Eliana's two-storey house catches my eye. I can hear the deep, hollow knocks, even now. What if we'd just refused to let him in? What if we'd called the police instead of listening to Morgan?

"Chels?"

I conjure the last of my patience. "Jordan wasn't there that night. He didn't see..." Steven with the knife. The knife he jammed in Morgan's chest. I held her hand while she choked to death on her own blood. I shake the image away and fight to focus on Cam again. "He can choose what he wants to believe. I can't control that."

I can only control myself, and acknowledging that simple fact gives me the power I need to get through this anniversary memorial one last time.

Cam squeezes my hand and I pull away. I look back at the house. Beyond the fence, a small group holding white rose stems gathers by where the peony bushes used to be —Ellie's favourite. I have to focus on who I am to these people. I have to be who they think I am. That's all that matters for today. Just today.

I open my purse to find my sunglasses, desperate for the modicum of privacy they'll bring me, and my fingers glide along the white envelope inside.

It will all be over soon.

Cam says something, but I can't focus. My mind returns to that night. The night I've forced from my memory any time it arises. The night it all went wrong. The night the blood stained my hands, too.

2

PAST

Shadows from the flames of a dozen white candlesticks dance along the walls of Lennox and Eliana's dining room. As I twirl the spaghetti around my fork, a garlic aroma wafts toward me. An acoustic version of a rock song I can't quite place plays from the speakers in the kitchen beside us as Lennox walks through the archway, another basket of cheesy garlic bread in his hands. He places it in front of me with a wink and scoots behind his sister, Eliana, to his seat between her and John.

In that moment, it hits me that if it hadn't been for the Halloween party, we all might never have met. It's strange how you can live in the same region, but if you went to different schools like we did, your paths might not cross.

John always sits at the head of the table. It's a spot he naturally took, and it suits him. If he hadn't introduced himself to me at the Halloween party last year, we'd all never have met in the first place.

"Would you pass that my way when you're done?" John nods to me with a perfect white smile from the head of the table as I take a piece.

I hand the basket to Morgan on my left, and she takes a piece before passing it to John beside her.

"I'm glad you came this time." John's fingers connect with hers before she lets go, and they exchange grins, matching pink flooding their cheeks. John takes a piece and sets the basket down in front of Eliana. She peers in, gives a quick, sad glance to Lennox, and picks out the last piece of bread.

"You enjoy," Lennox says, waving it away.

She tugs the crusty bread apart, the cheese holding on by a string as she places half on her brother's plate. His grin lights up the room more than the candles.

The trill of a ringing phone echoes from the front room, somewhere by the front bay window facing the water.

"That's me." Morgan says apologetically, hopping up, and disappearing into the far end of the pitch-black room. "I'm so full!"

I shove the forkful of pasta into my mouth and take a bite of the bread to go with it, my jeans tight against my stomach.

John rests his fork on his plate and eyes his bread, glancing into the living room before fixing his gaze on me. "You stress eating again, Chels?"

I swallow the last of my bite and press my lips together, staring at my empty dinner plate, my fourth piece of garlic bread still in hand.

I guess I am.

"What's up?" he asks.

I feel their eyes on me, heat rising to my own cheeks. I lean back in my seat, wondering if I should have confided in them about my stress binging.

John wipes his fingers on his napkin and lowers his voice. "I'm sorry, Chels. Maybe I shouldn't have mentioned—"

"It would have been my dad's birthday today." I pick apart my piece of bread, focusing on it as if it's the last morsel of comfort I might have—until my next meal. "It would have been his sixtieth."

"Wow." John nods, balling his napkin in his fist. "I remember when Murray would have turned thirty. It's funny how those milestone birthdays make you think." His gaze drifts to one of the candles until Morgan comes back in the room, phone in hand, and plunks down in her seat. John's gaze finds her again, magnetized like it's been the whole night.

"Sorry," Morgan mutters, setting the phone beside her plate. "What did I miss?"

"Chelsea's dad would have been sixty today," Ellie says.

Morgan gently grabs my arm and squeezes it with an apologetic look. "I'm sorry. I should have known that."

I shake my head and cover her hand with mine. "No, it's not even important. I barely realized. I don't know why it's getting to me like this..."

"Because even though he was a shitty father most of the time, you know it was the alcohol and trauma in his early life that made him that way." Lennox lifts his glass of red wine, resting his elbow on the table. "You have empathy, but besides that, we can all still mourn what we didn't get to experience with them—hell—even what your brother and your father didn't get to experience themselves. Ellie knows," he turns to her, "I talk about how Mom never got to see her thirtieth birthday." He mutters "addiction" before taking a sip from his glass. "Brought us together, and for good reason. If we can't talk about it with each other, who else will listen to this shit?"

John lifts his beer bottle and nods to him. "Before you guys, all I had was Austin." He stares across the table at the empty seat that Austin took when he made an appearance. "And you know he's not much of a talker." He and Lennox chuckle. "He listens though—when he's around. Sometimes, that's all we need." He gives me a warm smile. "We're here for you, Chels."

I smile and place my pieces of bread on the plate. "I know."

John stares down at the pieces and purses his lips, sighing. "I didn't mean to make you stop..." His voice trails off as Morgan's phone vibrates against the wooden table over and over.

"It's fine," I tell John before leaning over to Morgan. "Is it *him*?"

She nods. I want to take her phone and chuck it in the toilet. Maybe into Lake Ontario—it's just across the street. Anywhere to protect her from the creep on the other line.

"Dessert is later," Lennox says, catching my attention as we lock eyes. "Right now, I feel like dancing."

I huff a laugh, trapping it in my mouth. I can't stop studying him, trying to decide if he's joking or not. "I didn't know you danced."

"He doesn't," Ellie says. "He has no rhythm."

"She's right." Lennox laughs and sets his wine glass in front of him, still staring at me. His black dress shirt hangs off his slim frame, untucked and wrinkled in a charming sort of way. "Ellie got the co-ordination. Stole it all from me in the womb." He pokes her side and she bursts out laughing, finally taking his focus off of me and onto her as he beams with pride at the reaction he caused.

Morgan's phone vibrates on the table again. John casts a glance at Morgan before resting his gaze on me. He called me last night, asking if she'd be coming this time. I told him she would, including the fact that she'd finally broken things off with her boyfriend. I knew what I was doing—giving him the greenlight to pursue her. He'd been interested since I introduced them almost a year ago. He might have even stopped pursuing her out of respect for our friendship if I'd asked him to—that's just the kind of friend he is. I want Morgan to move on, and in truth, they'd make a great couple.

John is everything Steve's not.

Steve has been best friends with my brother since elementary school. I never liked him. He's pompous, obnoxious, cocky, cruel, and in relationships, it turns out he's a controlling asshat to boot.

John is down to earth, modest, and says he got his calm confidence from his late older brother, Murray. It separates him from anyone who awkwardly attempts to steal the spotlight, or own the room. John doesn't compete with anyone but himself.

Morgan's been my best friend since elementary

school. If not for that, maybe she'd never have gotten together with my brother's best friend. It's like I'm obligated to set her up with someone better. Her connection to me led her to a mentally and emotionally abusive relationship with Steve. Maybe this one will lead her somewhere healthy—happy for once.

Morgan came with me the first time we all met for support, but after hanging out with us a few times, Steve made it clear he didn't like her going without him. She's only joined me a few times since. Now that they've split, I'm glad she's back, and I know I'm not the only one.

John studies her as she bites her lip, clutching her cellphone in her fist. Just by looking at me, John can tell whatever's going on is bad.

"Do you want me to answer it?" I blurt over the annoying ring. "You know I'll tell him where to go."

"No," she says on exhale. "I just let it go to voicemail."

"Is it your ex?" John asks.

Morgan chews at her lip, with her face hidden behind her long, highlighted fringe, and gives me a wide-eyed look that asks what I've told him. I shrug with a smile and grab her phone.

"Hey," she laughs.

I hold the button on the side while staring at her. "There. Off for the rest of the night, okay?"

Morgan nods and settles back into her chair. I wish it were enough to ease her mind, but I know she's still on edge—waiting for his next move to coerce her back or shame her for leaving in the first place. So am I.

"Now that *that's* taken care of." Lennox inches around the dining table, grabbing a candle in each hand and brings them to the front room. He sets them by the bay window and his shadowy outline faces us. "Who's joining me for a dance?"

I toss my napkin on the table and stand. Ellie shoots me a pleased but shocked look. John and Morgan wear similar expressions.

"I'm not really in the mood to dance." I pick up my plate in one hand and Morgan's in the other, staring at her. "But I'll wash the dishes if you dry."

I want a chance to talk to her about Steve. He can't keep harassing her like this.

"No," Lennox calls. "You're not getting away that easy. The dishes can be done later. I want to enjoy my time with friends."

I ignore Lennox. Ellie grabs the other dishes and follows me to the kitchen. I'm not in the mood to make a fool of myself dancing in front of Lennox...

"How about it?" I hear John ask softly as I enter the kitchen.

Ellie and I glance at each other once we're out of sight and she peeks into the dining room from the alcove.

"Is she going to dance with him?" I hiss.

She nods before joining me at the sink.

"Good." I set the dishes down by the sink. "Anything to take her mind off her ex."

She takes the plates from me and rinses them under the tap. "When did they break up?"

"A couple weeks ago? He's been calling and texting every day since."

Eliana raises her brows and twists the knob, turning the water off. "Seriously? Like this?"

"It's pretty bad." I gather the pieces of my garlic bread and toss them in the compost. "Morgan says he'll stop, but I know this guy. He's relentless when he wants something. He's so entitled."

Ellie leans back against the counter and twists at one of her many gold rings. "How long were they together for?"

"Since the end of high school."

She gawks at me, her mouth agape. "That's almost a decade."

I nod as she pushes herself off the counter. "I don't know how she stayed with him so long. She never listened to me when I told her she should leave him."

"Huh." Eliana stops by the speaker on the island countertop, reaching for it. "What ended it?" She rests her hand on the knob of the dock, waiting for my answer.

A cold shiver descends my spine as three words come to mind.

I don't know.

She told me she was finally done with him, but something happened—something pushed her over the edge. If he'd hit her—hurt her physically—I'd have to believe she'd tell me... unless she's ashamed...

"I don't question it," I say, shaking the thought away. "I'm just glad it's over."

Ellie nods, seeming to consider that, and then turns the volume up on the speaker. "Come on," I think she says.

"Pardon?" I call over the music.

She grabs my hand and leads me into the dining room.

"No," I laugh, and try to pull away as she guides us into the living room, but her grip remains firm.

Lennox is strumming an air guitar as Morgan and

John dance with locked eyes, their giant smiles giving me a warm, tingling sensation.

"I can't," I laugh, finally pulling out of Ellie's grip.

"Yes, you can," Morgan says, grabbing my hand from behind me and twirling me around to face her. John laughs, watching as Morgan grabs my other hand and twirls us both around.

I wouldn't have danced for another soul in this moment; only for her. When I realized it would have been my father's birthday today, I hoped seeing my friends would cheer me up. Morgan's happiness is the perfect cure. I don't miss my dad, but I miss who he could have been to me. I miss the idea of having a dad. The kind of dad Morgan has, or that Lennox and Ellie talk about when they tell us about Simon, and how hard he tried to fill the roles of both parents for them.

In this moment, those thoughts and worries fade. We twirl around the living room, all of us, taking turns, until two pounds echo on the front door, loud enough to hear over the music. Loud enough that we couldn't have mistaken the sound for anything else, anywhere else.

We freeze.

"Is Austin coming?" Lennox asks John.

He shakes his head. "Not this time..."

Ellie leans into her brother and says something before heading toward the kitchen.

Lennox passes me on the way to the door, his spice and cedar scent lingering behind him. The music stops. Ellie reappears from the alcove in the kitchen. We all wait in silence.

Who could be here at this hour? A neighbour,

complaining about the noise? A friend of Lennox or Ellie's?

I walk beneath the archway, toward the hallway to the front foyer, exchanging a furrowed-brow expression with Ellie. Lennox stands in the open doorway, dead centre, staring into the night.

3

The moment I step out of the car, I feel all their eyes on me, cool as the breeze from the waterfront. They stand in small groups on the other side of the picket fence, speaking in hushed voices, likely about me. If I'd known who I'd become to them before I decided to give my witness statement and testimony in court, maybe I would have chosen different words. Maybe I'd have stuck to the facts of what happened that night.

Maybe it wouldn't have mattered.

They say I'm the victim of the tragedy and a hero at the same time. I don't identify with either of those labels, but it's how I'm seen to everyone in Newcastle.

Time twists memories and eases the burden of denial. No one really talks to me about that night anymore—they rarely even bring up my friends—except for on these anniversaries. Time is a friend to the innocent and an enemy to the guilty. Time has put distance between that night and I, because I've done what it takes to carry on.

But time can't dull the pain. The rusty copper wiring that claws my insides, winding tightly around every part of me that could carry me forward. They cut into me each time I'm reminded of that night. Not even the Xanax can fully numb it. And I deserve it.

The mourners look at me with a mix of pity, reverence, and for some, ongoing grief from losing loved ones that night. Lennox and Eliana's father Simon owns their house now. The memorial is held here, every year. They stand in suits and dresses at a table decorated with the white roses, greeting everyone who passes the white picket fence. The gate I once stumbled through with blood-soaked clothes, never to see my friends again.

Cam joins my side, tucking his cell phone in his pocket. I give Simon a short wave before I turn to the beach. I've done my best to keep up appearances and be there for the families. They count on me to honour our loved ones—to represent them in some way—to offer hope that someone who went through such trauma carries on with life.

"I'm just going to take a moment here." I whisper, squeezing his arm.

He nods, having understood from the time we started dating that there's no room for him by my side when I'm like this. "Take your time. I'll wait by the table."

Wind blows through my hair as a car drives by slowly, likely trying to find a place to park among almost twenty others.

That night, Morgan drove me here. We'd come together, looking forward to dinner and a night on the beach around a bonfire. We'd walk across the sand with bottles and blankets, disappearing behind the tree line.

We were so eager to share and connect over the mesmerizing flames of fire, to support each other through all our troubles until only embers remained.

We couldn't have known how that night would end—but maybe we should have. Maybe it was just a matter of time until it all went to hell. I don't understand why I wasn't dragged there, too.

"Chels," Kellan calls to me. She crosses the road in a light pink, floral dress. Her long, chestnut hair blows in the breeze across her face, but it doesn't hide the small, pink pout of her lips. She hugs me and I give her a tight squeeze back. "Did you just get here, too?"

"Yeah. The Xanax is finally kicking in," I whisper, pulling some hair away from my face. She presses her lips together, unsure of what to say, and I fold my arms. "I just want today over with."

Kellan nods, but she stares back with a blank expression. There's no way she can fully comprehend what I just said, but she never pretends to understand me or what I've been through. It's what I love about her. Everything she knows, I've told her voluntarily, and it's made me comfortable to confide in her the most. I keep things from her about that night, which makes the painful ache of disconnect worse in these situations. She wouldn't speak to me again if she knew the truth, but I feel safest with her because she never questions me. She's the one I share the most with, and she always makes time for me.

I pull a strand of hair from my mouth again and motion toward the little groups gathered on the lawn. "I don't like the idea of them watching. It's like giving my pain an audience."

Kellan rests her warm hand on my back as we walk

along the road, parallel to the white picket fence. We've been friends since high school. We played soccer on the Newcastle community team for two years before I quit. We drifted a bit, and I got closer to Morgan again. Kellan knew Morgan, too, but they never hung out. They didn't mesh, and we never forced it. They filled very different roles in my life; Morgan and I loved to be around each other constantly. 'Connected at the hip,' her dad used to say. Even though she was *there*, she was often caught up in her own world and didn't have as much attention or time for me after Steven came around. Kellan and I didn't see each other as often, mostly just on soccer practice days when we'd play together, before I quit the team during high school, but I could always reach out to her for a chat, advice, an opinion, or help. She wasn't around much, keeping busy on the fencing team, track team, and as president of the yearbook committee, but she was always *present* for me. Most of my favourite memories were with Morgan, but I felt most seen by Kellan.

After high school, Kellan and I only got together over the holidays through college, and after I graduated, we fell out of touch for a while. We'd catch up a few times a year when I met John and Lennox. She never met my new group of friends, but made efforts to reconnect soon after the murders. She was there for me like the old days, at a time when I felt I'd lost everyone—even my brother. When we started working at the high school together, we became closer than ever before. She comes with me on this day, every year.

She links her arm through mine as we take our time arriving at the gate. "Is Oz still coming?"

"I think so."

Oz is one of my favourite people to work with and it became that way shortly after I met him when he was a new transfer at the high school– a guidance counsellor.

"That's nice." She squeezes my arm. "You guys have really gotten close, huh?"

I nod, letting the breeze soothe me as we approach the gate.

I haven't spoken much about that night to Oz—not that I do with anyone—but he seems to understand much of what goes unspoken with me. It's the opposite of Kellan, really. While she never pretends to understand, Oz has this knowing look he gives me, as if he can sense my thoughts and feelings.

Last week, we got some time to ourselves after a parent teacher meeting, when some of the faculty went to a pub in town. He seemed to understand my desire to get through the memorial when he invited himself to come. I agreed, but I'm still not sure how I feel about someone new being here. He won't know anyone except for Kellan. That could be awkward for some people. Maybe he's like me and won't need someone holding his hand during an event like this. Maybe it's the idea of having him *want* to be here for me that I like most.

Cam meets us at the gate with eight white roses in his hands, handing me four. "Careful. Some thorns weren't removed." He nods to Kellan and hands her the rest. "Here you go."

"Thanks." They exchange short smiles. Cam goes back to the table to retrieve flowers for himself.

Lennox and Ellie's dad, Simon, approaches, hands in his dress pant pockets. He stops before me. "How are ya, darlin'?"

I take a shaky breath in, but it's the only thing that shakes. Thank God for Xanax. "Hanging in there. How about you, Mr. Sharpe?"

"I told you. Call me Simon." He stares in my direction from behind his sunglasses before lifting them slightly off his nose and wiping the tears from the tops of his cheeks, where they pool in the hollow, fleshy cushions beneath his eyes. "You need anything, darlin', you come to me."

I know where his children got their sweet nature from.

"Thank you."

"You see me before you leave, will ya?"

"Promise."

He always asks to share a drink with me once everyone has left. Usually something strong, like whiskey or scotch. I've never refused him, and he doesn't know that it's the only alcohol I've had since I reached drinking age. I assume they're the first of many drinks he has the night of each anniversary. It feels like the least I can do. For the rest of the night, he drinks alone.

He separated from the twins' mom when she refused to get help for her opioid addiction. She became home-less, living on the street. She lost her battle with addiction when Lennox and Ellie were ten. Without a partner to share his grief, Simon's the one who needs me most on this day. It's always been bearable because he never asks any questions. He only talks about the twins, shares memories of them, and plays a few songs they loved.

One year, he played the acoustic rock album we'd listened to that very night, and when I asked him to change it, he did right away. I don't know if he understood why. I think he realized without me having to say another word, just like he knew his son was interested in me.

It's another of the things he never mentions, but it's implied in the way he looks at me when he talks about Lennox—different than Eliana—like he not only acknowledges the fine line between what was and could have been with us—he respects it. No one else knows. No one else does that, and it does something for me. It keeps me connected to Lennox in a way no one else can, and feeling close to him is something. Looking into Simon's eyes hurts, seeing Lennox there, but it's the kind of pain you can only earn with love.

Simon leaves us with four roses in his hands, walking toward the candlelight vigil by the front bay window. Kellan joins my side again and I scan the crowd, studying the eyes of those closest to me, watching for anyone who seems off—angry, even—for any signs of the person who sent me the note in my purse. They might be watching right now.

I take a shaky breath and finish scanning. There's no sign of Oz, and I feel a tinge of disappointment.

"That sweet man. Ugh. You're so strong, Chels," Kellan says, staring after Simon. "You don't have to be. We're here for you." She nods to Cam and he drapes his arm across my shoulders, squeezing me against his chest in agreement.

"Do you want to go ahead?" Cam asks, nodding at the roses in my hands.

He knows I prefer having a moment at the vigil with less people around. I break from them and continue across the lawn. I stop just before the bay window on the other side of the emerald cedar, where their pictures are placed meticulously around candles. Where we all lay white roses each year. Where Simon kisses his fingers and presses them against the glass before his children's faces.

Every year, the same pictures.

The same white roses.

The same secrets.

The same candles, burning bright, like they did that night.

Burning like the lights on the porch at the Halloween party, where I met John and Lennox for the first time.

Where it all started.

4

PAST

Glowing jagged teeth and wide eyes glare at me from each corner of the wrap around porch as I pass the jack-o'-lanterns surrounding the house. The scarecrow on the rocking chair facing the back woods is even scarier. I don't do well on Halloween. I don't like to be scared for fun and I don't understand people who do. I march around quickly, until I find myself back at the front door.

Hip hop music I recognize from a long-ago college bar crawl blares from the open windows, drowning out the crickets. The house sits on the acreage along the outskirts of Newcastle. There are no neighbours to mind the noise for miles down the road. The bass intensifies the pressure in my chest, squeezing air from my lungs as I lean against the wooden railing by the stairs.

Taking a deep breath of smoky fall air, I remind myself: Morgan wouldn't have left me. She's the only reason I came. Even Steve would get in shit from Jordan if my brother found out he left me alone at some costume party out in the country without a way home. Jordan's always been protective of me, maybe more now that we're adults. He'd never let Steve hear the end of it for abandoning me. That had to be enough of a reason for him to stick around.

So where are they?

I stop before the storm door as the music fades between songs, and the wind chimes ring in the breeze. Goosebumps cover my arms and exposed legs at the thought of having to do another lap inside among the stench of beer and obnoxious drunks waiting to start something—be it a game, a mess, or a fight. I don't want any part of it. I wish Morgan hadn't insisted on coming, but I know why she did. Halloween is her favourite time of year and going to a party is her only way to enjoy the night. Steve wouldn't have wanted to do a movie night with us watching *Hocus Pocus*. I wouldn't have tagged along on a date with them to a haunted house like he wanted. Morgan settled on this—we all did—but I wish I hadn't come.

Steve wouldn't agree to wear a couple's costume, so Morgan insisted we wear matching cheerleader costumes from *Bring It On*. I just look like a random cheerleader without her around, and I'm already out of place. I don't know anyone. It's cold out. I want to go home.

I walk toward the door as it opens, music blares, and a man in a Speedo bursts through. He holds a beer in each hand, scanning me up and down with a creepy smile.

"You're Chelsea?" he slurs.

I frown, staring at the bottle. "How'd you know?"

"Your friend Morgan said I should find you and keep you company." He wiggles his brows at me.

I fold my arms over my chest. "Could you tell me where she is?"

"She was makin' out with that guy, in the leather jacket? Who's he supposed to be?" I continue to stare at him with a blank expression until he takes a swig of beer and holds the other out until the cold glass touches my arm. I take a step back and he laughs, shaking his head. "She said you might be resistant. I promise, I don't dress like this all the time." He nods down to his Speedo.

I continue staring at him.

He sighs. "They were in the kitchen."

"Thank you." I uncross my arms and brush past him to the door.

"*But*," he says.

I swirl around and scowl.

"They went out back to the woods. So she told me to keep you company." He pushes the bottle at me again.

"No thanks. I'm going to find her," I push past him and scurry down the stairs, mumbling, "And then we're getting out of here."

As I round the side of the house with a view of the woods behind the home, it feels like the guy is following me. I squint at the shadows behind me, but no one's there.

I knew I'd be uncomfortable around a lot of drunk people. Why did I come? Why does it feel like he's still watching me?

I glance back and spot something in black. Someone in a Ghostface mask walking on the porch, in the same direction, parallel to me. They stop, staring at me as I walk faster, my chest tight with dread.

"You know," a guy's deep voice calls, and I jump. "You're the only other person here not drinking."

I stop and turn around.

The guy removes the mask and offers a small smile. His eyes sparkle by the porch light. His short blonde crew cut is messy from the mask he holds in both hands.

I shrug. "I don't drink."

"Yeah? I'm just not feeling it tonight," he says. He leans against the wooden railing, biting his lip as he stares at his mask in his hands. "So how come you're here?"

I shrug, even though he's not looking at me. "I got dragged here by a friend. You?"

"I've been to this party every year since high school." He looks up at me from beneath his brow, speaking in a low tone I can barely hear. "Tradition, I guess."

I take a few steps closer so I can hear a little better. "So, you know the host?"

The porch light glows beside his head. "Yeah, my best friend, Austin. He's the one in the Speedo."

I raise my brows. "That asshole?"

He laughs. "He's not so bad. Little stubborn. I guess he dragged me here, too."

"You didn't want to come?" I take a few more steps toward him and notice the sparkle in his eyes is gone.

"I came every year with my brother." He fiddles with the mask, eyes down. "He died last year."

"I'm so sorry." I stop in his shadow, able to see his sharp features and the sadness in his eyes.

He clears his throat and shakes his head, looking

down at the mask again. "It was his fault. He, uh, he had a problem with alcohol, and..."

I recognize the anger and hurt in his voice.

"My dad did, too." I fill the long silence and he looks up at me. Do I sound like him when I talk about my father? "Drank *and* died. Cirrhosis."

He nods once as he pushes off the railing. "Murray drove drunk for like, the hundredth time. Crashed. Least he didn't take anyone else out with him." The last sentence holds an ingenuine bravado and he begins to put his mask back on.

"I'm Chelsea." I extend my hand up to him.

He takes it and gives it a gentle shake in his rough hand. "John."

This isn't some idiot trying to hook up at a party like Speedo guy; this is someone whose vulnerability makes me feel like I can be vulnerable, too. I let go first, worried I've held on for too long. I laugh, pressing my skirt down as far as it can go.

Behind him, something creaks. He twists to face the figure behind him. It stands from the shadows of the porch, the rocking chair creaking behind it.

The scarecrow is real.

I gasp and stumble back. John laughs and shakes his head.

"Didn't want to interrupt your meeting," the scarecrow says in a friendly tone, "but can I join the club?"

John takes a step back, creating a space for him, glancing at me with a curious look back at the scarecrow as he speaks.

"My mom left when we were young," he says as he approaches the railing beside John, pulling the burlap sack off his face. His dark, messy hair hangs in his eyes until he sweeps it away with one hand, clutching his mask with the other. "She lived on the streets, got addicted to meth, and died before our eleventh birthday."

"Our?" John asked.

"I have a twin sister," he says to him before turning to me. "Lennox."

His deep brown eyes sparkle as he reaches his hand down and shakes mine. The sensation of being held and understood permeates our skin as when John and I connected. Lennox lets go first and shakes John's hand next.

"Is your sister here?" John asks. "She should be, for our first club meeting."

Lennox and I laugh a little.

"Nah. I actually came here on a date—a first date." He looks at us and chuckles before elaborating. "It didn't go well. That's why I've been hanging out here."

"Define *didn't go well*," I say.

"She brought me into the bathroom for what I thought would be a make out session, but instead, she hit a line of coke and wanted me to join her."

"Oh wow." John shakes his head, fussing with his messy hair. "On a *first date*?"

Lennox shrugs. "I just wish we hadn't come together. Same car. I'm just waiting until she's ready to go."

"Do you know Austin?" John asks.

"Who?" Lennox blinks at him and pushes out his bottom lip in confusion.

"The guy in the Speedo." I fold arms over my chest from the chill of the October evening. Lennox shrugs and I laugh, turning to John. "He hasn't had the *distinct pleasure*."

"Chelsea's not a big fan." John leans his elbows against the porch.

"I caught that." Lennox smirks at me.

I'm impressed he can read me already and has a firm grasp on sarcasm.

"We played football together, back in the day." John stares past me towards the woods, drifting into a far-off daze. "With my brother, too. Some of the best times we shared were on that field. Murray was never drunk when he played. He wasn't selfish, either—not on the field. He was my hero."

Lennox and I exchange a shy glance.

"And being here reminds me of him, being around all these drunk people, and I don't want to think about him tonight because… sometimes all I can remember is the last time I was with him. He was drunk, just crushing beers on the back porch before he went out that night. He asked me to go with him to some party, but I said no. I hated being around him when he was so sloppy, and crude, with no regard for anyone else. I just left him there, drinking alone. That image is stuck in my head. Just Murray, drinking alone." John shakes his head, slaps his palm against the wooden porch railing, and stands up straight. "Don't mean to be a downer, guys."

"No. I can, um. I can relate." I clear the emotion from my throat and tuck my hair behind my ear for comfort as they both watch me. "My last memories of my dad were when he was dying in the hospital. He wasn't drunk anymore, but he was just a shell of who he used to be.

And it hurt." Emotion rises in my throat, and I clear it again, turning to John. "It hurts to see them like that—"

"Chels!" Morgan calls from somewhere beyond where the light from the porch touches the back lawn.

I squint to find her figure, stumbling from the trees.

"Told ya she'd be fine," Steve's voice echoes from somewhere further.

I roll my eyes and return my attention to John and Lennox. "I've gotta go."

"Let me get your number," Lennox says, digging his phone from his pocket. "Both of yours. You guys local?"

I nod and he passes me the phone to put my contact information in.

"I'm in the city," John says, "but I'd be down to hang out."

"I've got this place on the waterfront in town. My sister and I just bought it together. It's huge; a fixer upper. That's the only reason we could afford it. I'd love to have you by. Have a real first meeting, with Ellie, too."

"Chels!" Morgan releases a drunk burst of laughter, opening her arms wide as she stumbles toward me. Steve tugs her skirt down as it flies up in the breeze.

I pass the phone to John and nod to Lennox. "Sounds good. Just text me."

"Will do." Lennox nods as I start to walk away. "Nice to meet you. Didn't mean to scare you. This is just for the crows... and the girl in the bathroom." He winks.

I release a little chuckle and wave to them both. "Nice to meet you guys."

"Get home safe," John calls as he hands the phone back to Lennox.

Morgan wraps her arms around me, laughing in my

ear as Steve stops a few feet behind her with an unim-
pressed look at the guys on the porch.

"You're not mad at me, are you?" Morgan asks.

"Why would she be mad?" Steve stands behind her
and wraps his arms around her waist. "You're not her
babysitter. You're not responsible for holding her hand.
Chels is a big girl. She can handle herself."

I sneer at him and rub at Morgan's cheek where her
red lipstick is smeared. Steve must have seen it. He was
just going to let her walk around like this.

"She's a mess, huh? Time to go, messy pants. You
know, next time, you're wearing pants. This is just...
what?" Steve stares at my costume. "A cry for attention?"

"You're a dick," I say, hoping John and Lennox are too
far away to hear him. I reach for Morgan's hand and she
squeezes mine with a smile.

"Girls who dress like this any time of year scream
daddy issues." Steve shakes his head. "Somehow, you all
think on Halloween, it doesn't count."

He grabs Morgan's other hand and pulls her away
from me, propping her up under his arm. Her eyes don't
focus as she stares back at me. I wonder if she can even
hear what he's saying, or if it ever hurts her like it hurts
me—it occurs to me that he's never so brash around my
brother. Funny how that works.

"Let's just go." I grumble and lead the way back to
the car.

I look back over my shoulder. The porch is empty,
except for the glowing jack-o'-lanterns.

I wonder if Lennox will call, and if we'll really get
together sometime. If being around people who've experienced deep loss because of addiction might somehow

strengthen us—give us an outlet to vent and relate to each other—or even heal us.

I think it might be possible—but not likely. It was probably just a couple of nice guys, happy to connect, if only for a little while. Even now, with them out of sight, I wonder if it even happened. It feels like a dream.

I step onto the driveway leading toward the road as an odd grunting noise comes from somewhere close. To my right, the guy in the Speedo, John's friend, Austin, is bent over, hurling in the bushes.

"Gross," Morgan slurs, pressing her fingers to her red lips.

Steve and I exchange a wide-eyed look. When Morgan hears someone else being sick, it makes her sick, too. With no time to spare, we rush her past the bushes and onto the street. We load Morgan into the backseat of the car and Steve walks to the driver's side.

"Hey," I call to him. "Have you been drinking? Should I drive?"

"Nah," he shoots back, irritation in his tone.

"Are you sure—"

"You want all the reasons I'm not letting *you* question *me* alphabetically? Categorically? In order of importance?" He rests his hand on the top of the car. "I had one drink. You're a terrible driver. This—" he smacks the roof, "Is my car. Your place is in the back, Thompson. Remember that."

"Asshole," I call before sliding in beside Morgan.

She doesn't need to deal with us fighting again. I reach for the door to close it and my cellphone vibrates in my bag beside me. I take out my phone and there's a text from an unknown number.

Lennox here. Meet me at my house, the first Sunday of November. 306 Waterfront Road, Newcastle.

"Close the door! It's cold!" Steve shouts as the engine grumbles to life.

I slam the door shut with a smile and put my phone away. Then, I cozy up beside Morgan for the ride home.

5

I'm missing.

It's the thought I always have when I look at my friends' photos by the bay window. The glowing candles reflect in the glass frames and amplify the nostalgia. It's not that I should have been part of the photos, but that I should have been there, in the house when it happened, instead of walking by the water.

I should be dead. I've played out the scenario in countless ways. Sometimes, I imagine I'd be able to stop Steven from hurting my friends by distracting him—keeping his attention on me before he got violent. I wouldn't have been able to deescalate it, I never could, but I was the only one who ever confronted him on his bullshit. I wouldn't have been above threating to call my brother. If there was one person Steven was loyal to, it was Jordan, and if it got that bad, I'd do it. It makes sense that Jordan can't believe Steven killed my friends. I don't blame him for that. He always saw the good in Steven.

Most of the time, I imagine dying with them.

If I had, Steven would have gotten away—maybe for good, without any witnesses. He'd have gone on being best friends with my brother, all the while knowing he killed us.

There's no scenario where Jordan and I remain close.

Cam's efforts to bring Jordan here today were benevolent; his intentions always are. But I don't want to see Jordan. Not today.

I scan the crowd for Oz, but I don't see his dark, curly hair amongst those gathered. It isn't lost on me that Oz looks a little like Lennox. I might be attracted to him for that reason. It's the reason dating Cam was easier. He looks nothing like him, sounds nothing like him, and doesn't ever remind me of Lennox or what could have been.

Faces in the small groups of people gathered on the lawn watch me as I focus my attention back to the photos. If the person who sent me the note in my purse is here, they're watching me right now. Are we both wondering the same thing—what we're going to do?

Instead of taking another look through the mourners, I concentrate on the faces of those I loved.

I set a white rose before a picture of John from his high school football days. That was the year he claimed was the best of his life—when he played on the team with his brother.

Images of his smile flash before me. John, dancing in the living room with Morgan. Passing the bread basket to Ellie with candlelight shining in his eyes.

His breath heavy as he stumbled back from the

bonfire, losing his footing in the sand. The pain flashing in his eyes.

In the bedroom, the bloodstain pooling on his chest. His hand reaching for Morgan's.

I blink back tears, take a few deep breaths, and turn to the photo of Ellie and Lennox. Their arms are wrapped around each other, keeping warm on a cold Toronto night outside of a concert venue.

Ellie's solo close-up picture sits beside it. I place another rose. I can almost feel the warmth from her brown eyes. It feels like her appraisal when Lennox first introduced us. She wore a bohemian blouse, eclectic rings on most of her fingers, her hair tied in an effortless bun. She was the image of peace and joy from the moment we met.

Ellie in the kitchen, turning up the music, pulling me with her to dance—making meaningful moments from nothing. Her concerned face as her brother answered the knock on the door. Her oversized wool sweater falling from her shoulders as she ran through the sand on the beach, laughing as the incoming night tide hit her bare feet, turning toward us with confusion in her eyes. No, not at us.

Past us.

Ellie in the hallway, her trembling, crimson hand reaching for me as I slid through her blood to be at her side, straining to hear the last words she ever said—the ones she whispered to me as she gasped her last breaths.

Warm hands clasp each of my arms and I jump, startled, as Simon leans in toward my ear. "Sorry, darlin'. Don't mean to interrupt. We're going to say a few words once you're finished. You take your time. As much as you need." He squeezes my arms as if to say *I love you*. Simon's hands share their DNA. I choke on my tears and he sniffles, curses under his breath, and steps away.

Lennox's kind eyes are nearly hidden behind his curls in a photo from public school. Those eyes. That smile. I search for my favourite one and find him playing the guitar. I lay a rose before the photo and my lungs expand, full of the love I had for him that has no place to go anymore, and I'm no home for it. I wipe away tears. Lennox with his complex stare, always thinking about something; mischievous, knowing, and true.

Lennox in the living room, dancing close to me, neither of us wanting to take the chance and reach out for the other, but the hum of chemistry still undeniably there between us. He always ignited a buzzing sensation of joy when his eyes were on me, and I basked in his attention when I had it. Lennox at the door, staring out into the night. Lennox sitting by the fire, his deep brown eyes filled by it. The warm glow of his skin radiating tension as I took a seat beside him, only to catch Ellie's confused gaze moments later.

Lennox, stepping between me and the commotion. My protector.

Lennox in the living room, sitting on his couch in the shadows, his favourite record playing. His throat slit, wearing blood on his shirt like a bib. Lennox's eyes closed, apart from his sister—his soulmate—and so much left unspoken between us.

Lennox. He never saw it coming.

I press my hand over my mouth, stifling a deep cry as

the images flash before my eyes over and over, despite me closing them. Someone's hand is on my back, rubbing it, but it's not Lennox, and I want to shrug it off.

Get off of me, please.

I turn around and Morgan's mother holds her arms out to me. I fall into them, breaking down in tears as her dad watches on, his chin quivering. He avoids eye contact with me but covers my hand on his wife's back with his.

I've known them since kindergarten. Known Morgan since...

Her mom takes a thoughtful step back, nodding to me once, giving me space. In the collection of photos, I find my best friend's face. Her two front teeth are missing in the one I land on, and it hurts to see her that way, since I'm one of the few here who remember her like that. I find the picture of us with our cheerleading costumes on —the one we took before the party—and lay a rose beneath it. The memories of our friendship flood in with her gentle laughter as a backdrop. It's interrupted by a phone ringing.

Morgan's phone ringing. She puts it on silent; that won't stop him.

Morgan, dancing with John by the fire. I hadn't seen her that happy in a long time. Never with a man.

He won't stop.

Morgan on the beach, fighting to be heard over the shouting. Morgan in the bedroom, beside John. Her arms are folded over her bloody chest. Blood bubbles from the corner of her mouth as she stares up at me, eyes full of fear, unable to speak.

I think she was trying to warn me.

Watch out.

He's still here.

It's not over.

"Babe?" Cam's voice scares me as he steps beside me and takes my hand in his. "You ready?"

I clear my throat and nod, wiping tears from my cheeks as I put my head down and let him lead me away from the photos, toward the cedars beside the bay window where Morgan's parents have gathered with John's father, and Simon. We stop in front of them, taking my usual place by the families, and I wonder where John's mom is.

"Thank you all for joining us on the fifth anniversary of our beloved ones' passing," Morgan's father says, holding his wife's hand. "If you haven't yet received a white rose, please take one and pay your respects." He waves his hand toward the bay window. "They are a symbol of peace and pure love—the love we have for our daughter, Morgan, and that we have for Lennox, Eliana, and John. And for Chelsea." He adjusts his glasses, and I clench all my muscles—including my hand around Cam's—as he reaches the part of the speech I dread most. I never know how much he'll credit me for what I did that night—for what they think I did—but the attention builds to a point of sickness within me. Some years are worse than others.

"Chelsea was there that night, trying to protect them as best she could. She was there as some of them took their last breaths. She was there to make the phone call that would put an end to the life of the monster who took them from us. She filled in the gaps we needed. She gave us the closure we needed. Chelsea, on behalf of the families," he nods to the other parents and they nod back, "and our community, thank you for what you did. You're a brave woman and you continue to show us how to rebuild from tragedy, and to honour the lives lost by living your life with grace and love. May the innocent souls of our loved ones rest in peace..."

I can't handle it anymore. I can't pretend. But I can't leave; I don't get to walk away. My heart races and I shake my hand loose from Cam's, wrapping my arms across my chest to warm myself from the chills rolling off the water behind us.

Don't look back.

No one's there.

They're all dead.

I squeeze my eyes closed as Kellan wraps her arm around me, supporting me as I prepare to lose myself in a flood of images.

It's Simon's turn to speak.

The beach. The fire. The dark puddles of blood. The knock at the door.

"No parent should ever lose a child. To lose my twins —in such a... a brutal manner." I open my eyes as he presses his lips together. "No one," his voice shakes, loud for the whole crowd to hear. "Should have to go through this—but we have—we still are. We always will." His voice breaks and he cradles his head in his hands, sobbing.

I step out of Kellan's warmth and reach out to Simon, wrapping him in a tight hug.

"I'm sorry, darlin'," he gasps, rubbing my back.

He's comforting me, but if he knew the truth, he'd know I don't deserve praise.

I don't belong in the comfort of his embrace, but I will suffer through it, because I'm alive to do it, and to be here for the families. The last left alive, and the only one remaining to tell the tale. I told it well. Exactly as they would have wanted.

6

PAST

I clutch the sides of the blanket. I cannot recall when the officer sitting across the table from me wrapped it around me. I don't remember his name, or the name of the plainclothes detective standing in the corner, scrolling through her phone. My teeth are still chattering. It feels like I'll swallow my tongue at any moment, if I'm not careful. The officer told me the adrenaline was still running its course. I was having a panic attack. He reassured me I couldn't swallow my tongue. I believe him, but it doesn't stop me from trying to press it against the roof of my mouth to keep it in place. He told me to take my time answering questions. That it's normal to need more time to process.

Nothing is normal. My friends are dead.

I can think it, but my mind won't quite wrap around the concept. I saw it with my own eyes. I was covered in their blood. What feels like every few minutes, I check my hands, beneath my fingernails, sure I'll find some still there. It's been washed away, but I don't feel clean.

"Chelsea." The officer slides toward the front of his chair and folds his hands on the table dividing us in the small, cramped room. "Are you sure I can't get you a warm drink before we start?"

"I'm not cold. It's just the adrenaline, like you said." I grip the sides of the blanket and tug them close, clasping it with one hand while I give the other some relief. "I'm ready. I just want to start now, okay?"

I'm not ready. I want to leave my tongue pressed against the roof of my mouth. I want this over with.

The detective in the suit standing beside him nods, tucks her phone away in her pocket, and takes a seat beside me.

"We'll go at your pace, Chelsea." The officer leans back and looks to the woman.

"Start from the beginning," she says.

I close my eyes, trying to figure out where that was. It started the night I met John and Lennox, but that's not what they mean. They want to know about tonight. Just tonight.

"Morgan picked me up from my apartment, and we drove to Lennox and Eliana's place."

"At what time?" the woman asks.

"Dinner was for seven, so we got there just before that. Lennox, Eliana, and John were there already. We had dinner, had some drinks, and there was a knock at the door."

"What time was that?" she asks.

"I don't know... around eight thirty, maybe."

"Who was there?" the officer asks. "At the door?"

"No one. No one was there when Lennox answered."

"Go on."

I take a deep breath. The back of my neck prickles with goosebumps, thinking about him. "Steve was calling Morgan, trying to talk to her." I've never called him by his full name, but Steve sounds too informal, too personal for what happened. Steve is the name you'd call a friend. "He called multiple times—I don't know how many—until she turned her cell phone off. He did that a lot since they broke up."

"And when was that?" the woman asks.

"Recently. I don't know *exactly* when. I don't even know what finally made her do it. She complained about him a lot for a while, and I'd tell her to leave. Then, I complained about him a lot, and she didn't like that, so towards the end of their relationship, she didn't talk to me about him much." The look she gave me, like *I* was the one who'd hurt her, who did something wrong. "Even though they were broken up, he wouldn't leave her alone." She finally saw him for who he really is but it was too late. "She tried to get a restraining order against him. I came with her that day, to this police station, but *you* wouldn't do anything about it. You said there was no *imminent threat of danger*." Tears burn my eyes. I struggle to take a full breath and clench my fists. "We were scared of him—of how far he'd go—and we tried to tell you—"

"We'll check the records of that, Chelsea, but for now, we need you to tell us what happened tonight—"

"I'm telling you what happened! You failed her! We all failed her and now they're all dead!"

The woman rests her hand on my arm and I yank it away, pressing my lips together. I stare at her wide-eyed, but my gaze falls to the table as flashbacks of the evening flood in.

The officer across the table holds his hand up to the woman and looks at me. "Chelsea, breathe in for three seconds, hold it for three, and then out for three, okay? Do it with me."

I inhale, shaking, tears spilling down my cheeks, dripping off my chin. I regain control, one breath at a time.

"Chelsea," the woman interrupts us. "I'm very sorry for what happened to you and your friends." She rests her elbows on the table before us and folds her hands together, careful to keep some space between us. "We want to make sure justice is served for all of them."

"There is no justice." I shake my head, my focus back in the present. "Steven's dead. He can't—" I swell with anger and push the blanket off my shoulders.

The cool air on my skin is unwelcome.

"We need you to tell us what happened," she says.

"Steven came to the house, he was drunk, he demanded to see Morgan, and so—so aggressive. He kept trying to come in and Lennox wouldn't let him, but Steven would bounce off of Lennox, like he was ready to fight. They kept him out until Morgan told them to let him in."

"Them, who?"

"Lennox and John. They were blocking the door until Morgan said she wanted to hear him out." I press my fingers to the moisture around my eyes and apply it to my temples, pressing against the ache in circular motions. "I told them not to, but they didn't listen to me. The way Steven—the way he looked at me when he came in—like *I* betrayed *him*." I shake my head. "I told Morgan—I told her if he stays, I'm leaving." Lennox tried to grab me, reason with me, but I stared into Morgan's eyes. "She didn't say anything to me. She just turned her attention to Steven and they went down the hall toward the back bedroom. And I left."

"You left." The officer frowns. "Did you have reason to suspect he would be violent with Morgan? With anyone?"

If they tried to make him leave, maybe. He might have fought them—most likely John—but before then, he'd only ever fought kids at school. That was years ago. He'd never physically hurt Morgan, that I knew of. It was one of the reasons she couldn't get a restraining order.

Was it the reason I left tonight?

No.

I didn't leave because it felt safe leaving them. It felt too unsafe to stay, because I've been there before—with men like Steve—like my dad. I didn't want to stay and see how it ended.

"I think I knew things could get bad. I didn't want to be there—" I left, like a coward.

My arms shake as I cling to the blanket. I left them. I never should have left.

The officer nods. "Did you see or hear anything else before you stepped out?"

I shake my head.

"Was he previously abusive to Morgan?"

"Emotionally, yes. Very. But he never hit her—that I know of. But the things he said to her and the way he tried to control her—he'd get angry when she went against him, and when he unleashed on her... well, he's snapped before. He threatened that she'd be sorry if she didn't give him another chance. That wasn't enough for you." I sneer at them. "I'm sure it's still in her voicemails.

You got to hear it before, but I guess now," my voice quivers with anger, "you'll pay a bit more attention when you hear it again."

"When you left, where did you go, and for how long?" The woman asks.

"I went down to the beach across the street and took a walk by the water. I don't know for how long, but when I went back, I thought he might have left by then. Half an hour? It could have even been an hour. I really don't know. I called the police within minutes after I got back, though."

The officer and the woman exchange a look.

"People saw me. A woman walking her dog. She must live close. A couple was walking down the street on my way back. I passed them when I crossed."

"And what happened when you returned?"

I frown, squinting as I did when I tried to see if his car was there on my way back.

"Chelsea?"

"I didn't notice Steven's car when I left. When I got back, I was looking for it, but I didn't see it. I thought he was gone..."

"We found his vehicle parked around the corner," the officer says.

I turn to him. "Like he didn't want us to know? Like, maybe he knocked on the door the first time, and left, and came back?"

"We can't speculate right now," the woman says. "Please, continue."

"I was going to knock, but... I felt like I had to swallow my pride walking back in there after I'd stormed out.

When I went in, it felt as cold as outside. Something was off. I thought maybe they'd had a big fight and Morgan was upset, and that's why it was so quiet. I walked into the space between the living room and dining room, and I saw Lennox first. He was on the couch, but I didn't realize his... his neck..."

"Deep breaths," the officer says.

I listen to him, but tears flow freely once again. I remember his tilted head and the blood down his shirt. I press my tongue to the roof of my mouth. I won't swallow it. I can't. It feels like I will. It feels like I'm going to die.

"Keep going, Chelsea."

"When I realized what happened to him, I was shocked. I went toward the bedroom and that's when I saw her. Ellie. She was lying on the floor in the hallway, in a pool of blood. She'd been stabbed in the chest. I thought—I thought she was dead. As I got closer, she made a gurgling noise and I can't stop—can't stop hearing it." I press my lips together to stifle my cries.

"Take your time," the officer says.

I squeeze my eyes shut, but all I see is Ellie staring up at me, helpless and dying.

"I dropped down beside her, and I grabbed her hand. She pulled me in close and whispered to me. I was so scared. That's when I knew." The goosebumps cover my arms again and I shake off the shiver of knowing. The blood from kneeling by Ellie is caked and congealed on my knees. "I knew he was still there. I realized what he'd done."

"Who?" she asks.

"Steven."

"Did you see him?"

I shake my head. "Not yet. I told her to hold on. I called 9-1-1 on my way to the bedroom. I knew Ellie didn't want me to go in there—or maybe she didn't want me to leave her—but I had to see about Morgan, and John. I entered the room and found them on the floor. John looked dead, but Morgan, she could hardly breathe, and blood was coming from her mouth." I cover my mouth as the image floods back. "I grabbed her hand and she... she shook for a bit, gasping, and then she died. She died holding my hand. They were all dead except Ellie, so I waited by her while on the phone with the dispatcher. She told me a car was on the way, but I knew if he was still there, I was in danger. I couldn't just leave Ellie alone, though." I speak quickly, racing to tell them what happened, desperate for them to know the truth of what we went through. "I went to her side again, and I pulled her close, and she died in my arms. I was in shock, and he brought me out of it. His boots. The sound of his boots on the floor as he stepped out of the bedroom. He was holding the knife in his hands." Bloody hands. "I was just in there, though. I don't know how he... was he hiding in the closet?"

No one has that answer for me. They don't know anything. Keep going. Almost done.

"I tried to get up, but I slipped in the blood. Steven came toward me, but we both heard the sirens. He hesitated, so I ran for the front door. He shouted my name, but he must have stumbled, maybe because he was drunk, or maybe he slipped in blood, too. I don't know. I got there first. I opened it and the police were pulling up.

Steven followed me out and they shot him. If they hadn't shot him..."

I'd be dead, too. I should be dead like them. I abandoned them because I was afraid. I couldn't handle that Morgan wouldn't listen to me.

"Did Steven say anything to you? Anything other than your name?" the woman asks.

"No."

"Did you say anything to him?"

I shake my head. "No. He shouted my name. That's it."

"How long had you known Steven Wilmot?"

"Since before kindergarten. My older brother, Jordan Thompson, met him in school and they became best friends."

"And that's how Morgan and Steven met?" the officer asked.

Through me. It's all because of me. "Yes."

"Did you have any reason to suspect Steven Wilmot was capable of physical violence?"

He'd never hurt anyone physically in front of me, but that's not what they're asking. They want to know if he *could* have done this. What don't they understand?

"Do I think he was capable? Yes. So did Morgan, or she wouldn't have tried to get the restraining order."

"Had anything happened in the recent past that might have instigated Steven? Set him off?"

"Set him off?" I ask the woman, my chest tight with frustration. "She wouldn't take him back. She was trying to move on with her life. You think *she* set him off? This is *her fault*?"

"I didn't say that. I just need to know if they'd seen

each other recently, met up another time after the breakup, perhaps, or if she had moved on. Was she seeing anyone else? Was Steven jealous of someone new in her life?"

I imagine Morgan and John dancing together, his hands on her hips. Hers around the back of his neck. She was happy again.

"They weren't officially together, but Morgan and John were interested in each other. There were feelings there." Faster than I'd have thought so soon after the breakup. "Saying Steven was the jealous type would be an understatement. He didn't like when she dressed showing too much skin. He didn't like when she spoke to other guys, except my brother, really, and he even discouraged her from hanging out with me because I was a *negative influence*." I choke out the last words. "He didn't want to see her with anyone but him."

He took so much from her—from us. "It was never enough for him, and I knew it wouldn't be. He wouldn't leave her alone until he got what he wanted from her, and they let him in. I should have tried harder. I should have shoved him out and locked the door on him. Who cares what they would have thought about me? They'd be alive. It's not their fault. It's mine. I couldn't protect her." My wide, burning eyes gloss over with tears, but I don't have enough for them to spill over. I want to cry, need to release this aching in my chest, but I can't.

"I left them there and he killed them because she wouldn't—I know she wouldn't go back to him. They— they wouldn't listen. There was so—so much blood." My chest heaves but I can't draw breath.

"Okay," the officer pushes his chair out and leans toward me. "Chelsea, let's take a break."

The woman stands. "Can I get you a drink?"

I can't breathe. I can't think.

They become a blur, and the room spins as the grey closes in.

7

Cam's strong hands rub at the muscles across my shoulders, easing the tension away in the dim light of our walk-in closet.

"That feels nice," I whisper.

He pushes his fingers up my neck, into my hairline, sending shivers down my spine as I release a soft moan. He kisses my neck and starts to unzip my dress but stops. His hot breath remains on my neck, closing in on my ear.

"Are you sure you won't come?" he asks.

My shoulders rise. He's trying to butter me up to go to his father's retirement party.

"I told you." I turn to him and take his hands in mine. "After today, I don't want to go anywhere. I just need to be alone."

And I don't want to be around law enforcement. Ever since that night, five years ago, their presence triggers fear in me.

"My family would love to see you there." He stares into my eyes, evaluating me as he does a puzzle, trying to create the piece needed to solve it, to make the image he wants to see. "Callie was asking about you the other day, and you know my dad would be so happy you came. I don't think you should be alone tonight, Chels."

He's only trying to help. Just a little while longer and I'll be on my own. Patience.

"I wish I could make you feel better. If I knew how, I'd do it for you right now. Whatever it took." His eyes fall away from me as he takes a few steps back.

"I wish it were that simple." I reach behind me to pull the zipper, but I can't reach it.

He returns to the floor-length mirror, straightens his tie, and clears his throat. "I don't know what time I'll be home."

"That's fine," I say, a little too quickly.

He raises his brow and shoots me a look. "If you need me, just call. I'll have it on vibrate."

"Thanks. Can you?" I point to my zipper.

He pulls it down gently. I hold the front of it against my chest as it falls away from my back. I take a deep breath and glance at the pajamas I'm eager to pull on. I'll dig a pint of ice cream out of the freezer, watch reality TV, and fall asleep on the couch so I don't have to be alone in our bed with my thoughts.

Cam will come home, collect me, bring me to our room, and cuddle with me until I fall asleep thinking of him—or nothing at all. Anything but that night, and what I have to do next.

"Thank you." I turn around and he's already gone.

After pulling on my pink satin shorts and cami, I twist my hair into a bun and walk downstairs, stopping in the foyer. I take the white envelope out of my purse, bringing it to the dark kitchen, lit only by the moon through the windows. I lean against the marble counter and slip the single sheet of paper from the envelope.

I tore the top of it off when I'd retrieved it from the mailbox yesterday after work, betting it was junk mail. When I unfolded the paper for the first time, my blood ran cold. It does again now.

They paid for what they did. Now it's your turn.

Tell the truth, Chelsea, or more will pay.

Tell the police the truth about what you all did that night or I will, and you'll lose what's left of your miserable life.

Shivers run up my spine as I absorb the words. A weight builds deep inside me—a heavy burden. Tell the truth about that night.

You have 48 hours to confess.

I brace myself against the counter, reading the sentences over and over. There's no time on the paper, but I know my deadline is tomorrow night. I have until tomorrow night to do what I should have done five years ago.

I tuck the paper back in the envelope. At first, I thought the sender to be one of Steven's defenders— those who believe he was innocent. Perhaps it was someone from an online forum, or a subreddit, where cracking cold cases is attempted.

As one of their prime suspects, they know more about me than I'll ever be comfortable with. They were dissatisfied with the interview transcripts, and the detectives' conclusions. Just like Jordan. They question the timeline, even though everything I said matches with the medical examiner's report. They wonder where I was for a half hour to an hour while my friends were slaughtered. They try to contact me, less and less now, but it still happens. They still think I know something that no one else does.

They're right.

I set the letter in front of Cam's office computer. I pull up a folder with pictures from my college days. The only picture I have of our group is a selfie taken on the beach by a bonfire from the first night we all got together. It was November; we were huddled together, bracing against the Lake Ontario chill.

I thought the letter to be an empty threat, but I couldn't stop wondering. What if it wasn't? If someone knows what we did that night, why haven't they gone to the police themselves? Why are they forcing me to confess?

What they wrote—it's not specific, but it's true.

What you all did.

I called a lawyer for legal advice. I told them what I was thinking about doing. I wanted to know what the consequences would be. They confirmed my worst fears, but assured me they'd fight to get me a better outcome, and limit the time I'd serve.

Clutching the letter, I glance at the bar cart by the window and my breathing slows. I stare at the liquor bottles on the cart. Whatever demons my dad numbed away while he drank multiplied *because* he drank. I won't do it. I won't bury myself any deeper than I already am. I'm barely above ground. I'm barely breathing.

It doesn't matter who knows what. I know what I have to do.

I stare into the computer screen, scanning my old friend's faces.

"What we did," I whisper, my chin quivering as tears

spill down my cheeks. "I wish I could take it back. I think —I think I'm finally going to do the right thing. I'm going to do what we should have done that night, as soon as we knew he was dead. I'm sorry."

Their faces stare at me, smiling, guiltless, and glowing by the light of the fire.

Even when I had them here, we couldn't agree on what should be done. Their opinions wouldn't help. Alcohol won't. Food never does. I have no one to talk to— no one who'll understand.

This letter. It's because of the anniversary. It has to be.

I learned how to push what we did way down deep inside in order to survive. I've done what I had to do to be free, but as I reread the letter over and over, one word stuck out more than any other.

Miserable.

My miserable life.

They're right.

I close the picture.

Nothing I've built is real.

I stand and shuffle out of the room, crumpling the note in my fist as I crawl into bed.

Tomorrow morning, I'll start my last day as a free woman. Then, I'll trade it for another form of freedom; that which frees me from the burden of lies, which have slowly been killing me for half a decade. I'll do this on my terms.

I open the drawer of my nightstand and shove the balled-up letter inside. I take a lightheaded deep breath and lay back against the stack of pillows on my side of the bed.

If the blackmailer had anything to go off of, they

wouldn't be threatening me. They'd have the power and control. They might think I'm scared to lose what I have, but in truth, I'm relieved. I wasn't supposed to carry this alone, and in some ways, it was easier. I close my eyes and press my cheek to the cool pillow.

But no matter how much I appeared to move on from that day, I've never been happy. Not really. It's been too long since I've known peace and I might never feel it again, but that's the price I have to pay. That's what my freedom costs.

As I drift into sleep, I resolve the remaining stress the way I always do.

I'm not a bad person. I did a bad thing. I'm not a bad person. I did a bad thing.

8

PAST

John and Morgan pass me in the hallway, holding hands. The cool draft of the evening caresses me as they go by. They reach the doorway where Lennox stands alone, looking out into the night, and Morgan links arms with him. They walk the pathway toward the picket fence, laughing as I remain behind with an uneasy feeling I can't describe.

Who was at the door? Don't they care?

"Here," Ellie says, handing me one of the two throw blankets she's carrying.

I take it and follow her outside, trailing the laughter from the trio ahead as Ellie shuts it behind us.

She links arms with me as we cross the street to the beach.

"Lennox doesn't like to talk about the good times we had with our mom," she says, staring ahead at him. "He's like our dad that way—but I do. I remember how she used to do my hair before dance recitals. How she was patient when it was always so knotted and tangled. She told me I was beautiful." She presses her lips together and releases a sigh. "I don't really get to talk about that much."

"You can talk to me about anything."

She smiles, her eyes glassy. "I know. Do you have any good memories about your dad on his birthday?"

I shake my head instinctively, but I pause, remembering when Jordan and I were young and mom and dad's side of the family got together to celebrate his thirtieth. They had a backyard barbecue. It's not really a memory, but we have it on VHS, and I've watched it a few times, trying to keep what I remember about my mom fresh in my mind.

"There was one time, but I was young. The family came together for a barbecue, and it was the first time I saw my dad being kind of shy. He always seemed so confident around us, but with everyone there, I think he was overwhelmed. He wasn't all that social, but he was happy. He smiled a lot, and when he made a speech to thank everyone for coming, he mostly thanked my mom. She was dying at that point, we all knew it. He told her how grateful he was to have her, and for the beautiful children she gave him, and he looked at me and my brother with real pride." A lump forms in my throat. "I don't remember ever seeing him look at me like that again."

"But for that moment in time, you were happy. You felt loved?"

I nod as we trudge through the sand, around the large rocks to the fire pit we set up at the beginning of summer. "I did."

"That's why it's hard for us, you know," she says, pulling me back a little to slow down as the others skip ahead. She pulls her hair into a messy bun. "We all felt love from them: your dad, our mom, John's brother. We all felt love and we all lost it, but it wasn't when they died. Not even John's brother. We felt it slip away as addiction took over. We've experienced more goodbyes than most." She tucks her arms under her blanket. "It's okay to be extra sad today. We're here for you."

I drape my arm across her shoulders and we stagger through the sand to the dried-out logs around the pit.

John crouches with his lighter while Morgan collects kindling from the tree line separating the houses on the street from the beach.

"What were you two whispering about?" Lennox asks, taking a seat on one of the logs.

"You two share that one," Ellie nods to the blanket in my arms and then at Lennox before sitting on the log on the opposite side with hers.

I know what she's doing. We both do. My cheeks flush as I sit beside Lennox, enough space between us so we're not touching, and offer him some of the blanket.

He pulls it across his lap and leans his elbows forward to rest on his knees. "John, let me know if you need help with that."

"I want to try," Morgan says, hiccupping with handfuls of dried bark. She joins John's side and shows him her findings.

John smiles up at her and hands her the lighter. "Go for it." He sits beside Ellie and takes some of her blanket with a grin.

"How's Austin doing?" Lennox asks.

John shrugs. "Haven't heard from him in weeks so, you know, the usual."

"Is he in Bali?" Ellie asks.

"That's the last place he posted on Instagram. I can't keep up. I wish I had the time and money to travel and not have to work."

"You know he's running from it," Ellie says. "His grief."

John nods quickly. "I'm sure he is. I'd love to run away from it all, too, but I have responsibilities. A house. A career."

"I get it—" Ellie starts.

"I know they were best friends, but Austin's always been flighty. He came in and out of my brother's life. He said he'd be here for me whenever I needed him. He said he'd be here for me..." He stares into the non-existent fire and presses his lips together, shaking his head.

I exchange a look with Ellie and Lennox.

We all heard Austin tell him the same thing every time he joined the group. He'd grip his shoulders, stare him straight in the eye, and promise to be there. He'd say he was just a call away or that he'd come and be with him if he ever asked, even if he was across the world, as he often was.

"I think he tries," Lennox says, watching Morgan light the kindling. "He's doing the best he knows. He hangs out whenever he's in town, right?"

John nods and shoves his hands in his pockets. "You're right. He tries."

There's animosity lingering in his tone as the fire from the kindling catches and races up the logs.

"Haha," Morgan laughs, clapping her hands. "Did it!"

"Nice!" I applaud.

Morgan gives John a little crooked smile as he wraps

his arm around her to help her stand. He sways a little, guiding her toward Ellie's log. Drunk and happy is fine by me.

As the fire grows, Ellie stands. "Just going to get my feet wet."

She walks toward the water, stopping to roll up the legs of her jeans along the way and we all watch her walk toward the moon, which hangs just above the horizon. John takes a swig from the bottle of wine and offers it to Morgan. She laughs and lets him pour some in her mouth. As it dribbles down her chin, John wipes it away with the sleeve of his shirt.

We have the whole beach to ourselves tonight, and I take a moment to be grateful for it as Ellie dances freely along the sand, her sweater slipping off one of her shoulders.

"They're cute," Lennox leans in and whispers to me. I nod and he stays close, his spice and cedar scent bringing comfort and excitement to my senses. "They're kinda perfect for each other."

"Yeah?" I watch Morgan take the bottle and a long swig of wine, making a mental note that I'll have to be the one that drives us home. "And what makes two people perfect for each other?"

"It just fits." The bronze glow of the fire casts light across his sharp features as he faces me. "He's a protector. He's a provider. Ever since we met, when he was looking after you at that party."

I frown. "He wasn't looking after me. He was following me in a Ghostface mask—"

"He saw you were alone in the dark at Austin's place.

He was looking out for you, whether you realized it or not."

"You know that for a fact?" I cock my head to the side.

He nods. "He wants to be the hero. Morgan might not need rescuing, but I think it's fun for both of them to play those roles. Big tough hero." John sets the bottle of wine down and turns back to Morgan with a grin. "Damsel in distress, finding someone who wants to help pick up the pieces after her breakup..."

I want to ask him if he thinks *we* would *just fit*, but instead, I follow his stare. John grabs Morgan's face in his hands and leans down, kissing her. Beneath the moonlight, too. Is there anything more romantic?

"That didn't take long," Lennox leans in closer to me and whispers with a laugh as I sigh.

I look away to give them privacy, watching the waves as Ellie walks along the shoreline, letting the water roll over her feet, splashing at her ankles. I think I hear her laughing, but the crackle of the fire drowns it out.

She turns around to face us with a smile, but it slowly fades. Does she see John and Morgan making out? I follow the direction of her confused gaze.

Steve emerges from the tree line, his stare fixed on John and Morgan with a clenched jaw.

What is he doing here?

How long has he been there?

He marches forward with balled fists.

9

Steve storms toward us as the fire grows, shouting, "Morgan!"

I stand, the need to intercept overwhelming as he nears the couple.

"Chelsea," he calls, turning his attention to me. "Chelsea!"

That's not what happened...

"Chelsea," Cam whispers, rubbing my arm. "Babe, you're crying."

My eyes flutter open in our dimly lit bedroom. I wipe my wet eyes and roll over with a sigh, pressing my hand against my chest, heart racing beneath it.

"I'm sorry I'm home so late," he whispers. "I'm going to change and then we'll cuddle, okay? You don't have to be afraid. I'm here."

I nod and sniffle, taking a deep breath as he pulls off his shirt and walks toward the closet.

The nightmares never stopped, but they're more sporadic, now. I'll always dream about that night, my guilty conscience calling me back to the time and place I betrayed myself.

"You know, I ran into Officer Pierce," he calls from the closet. "He was asking about you."

The officer who brought me in for questioning the night my friends were murdered.

"Oh?" My heart races as I recall what I can of that night I spent shivering uncontrollably in a blanket as I was questioned by Officer Pierce and the female detective.

"Yeah. Officer Whalen's about to wrap up desk duty."

Officer Whalen was the one who protected me that night, and paid the price for it. When he killed Steven, he strayed from the protocols and procedures he'd been trained on. He was suspended, and prohibited from carrying a service weapon for five years. Cam's dad told me that meant a lot of paperwork in the pit.

Cam flicks off the closet light and struts toward the bed, naked. As he closes in on me, his eyes fill with concern. He slides in beside me, and I roll onto my side away from him. My heart's racing again.

They paid for what they did, the letter says.

Is that what it was? Karma catching up with them? Then why not me? Why did I escape Steven's revenge massacre? I'll never know.

"Chels," Cam's gentle voice barely finds me. "I'm here if you need me. I'll always be here for you."

I take a deep, shuddering sigh and nod. I hope it's enough for him to know I appreciate him, but I can't speak with the giant lump in my throat.

Tell the truth. To finally tell the truth means sacrificing everything; not just what's left of my life, but to change the way my friends will be thought of and remembered. I'll take ownership of all of it. Maybe that's why I lived— to take responsibility for them.

"I know you don't want to talk about it," Cam says, "but I want to know how you're feeling."

"Not good, Cam. Okay?" I can't hide the edge from my tone.

"I know you went to therapy for a little bit, but maybe it's time to go back?"

Therapy hurt far more than it helped. I couldn't be honest about what I'd done, and the questions she asked made it impossible to block out the truth. When I started down that road, the feelings overwhelmed me to the point that I couldn't leave the bed for days, even though I barely slept. I missed time at work. I couldn't eat. After each session with her, I knew what would follow, and eventually I couldn't take it anymore. Without even understanding my situation, she was forcing me to face a truth I wasn't ready for. I couldn't own what I'd done. I couldn't face the pain I'd inflicted—and continue to inflict. In some ways, I still can't.

Tomorrow, I'll have no choice.

"Yeah. Maybe." I grip my pillow and squeeze my eyes shut, hoping he'll just stop.

"I was reading up on survivor's guilt, and it's common, and totally normal, Chels—"

"Cam. Please. Not tonight. Just not tonight."

He sighs and I sway on the mattress as he turns over, giving his familiar, informal resignation to the discussion.

He doesn't deserve this.

He deserves to truly know the person he promises forever to. It hurts to admit, to finally acknowledge that he loves me, but he doesn't know who I really am. He doesn't really love *me*. He loves the image of me, and I have no idea why. Once he knows the truth, he'll understand the wedge between us, and why I could never fully give myself to him.

An eerie calm settles over me and I turn over again, and wrap my arms around him. His warm hands find mine and he squeezes them.

Twenty-four hours to go—or more like twenty, now—to finish living this lie I've built. And then I'm free.

I take a deep breath, filling my mind with the ideas and plans I've prepared. I'll never see my brother again, though I've gotten used to that idea already. Not seeing my niece and nephew is hard—them knowing the truth is even worse. But Kellan won't have to bear the burden of supporting me. Neither will Cam. This is the last time I'll fall asleep beside him.

I press my body firmly against his and nuzzle my face into his neck.

"Hey." His voice becomes playful as I slowly graze my hand down his chest, across his stomach. "Hello, there."

I'm going to do this. I'm really going to confess. I'm so scared.

"I don't want to be alone right now," I whisper.

"Babe." He turns over toward me with a smile. "You're not alone. I'm with you. I'm right here," he says, and kisses me deeply. "I'm going to make sure you feel that—feel me—and never question that again."

"I need you, Cam."

One last time.

One more selfish act.

One more night of him seeing me as beautiful before the mask comes off.

Kissing me, he rolls over me, positioning himself between my legs. He pulls away from my lips until he's staring deep into my eyes, his hands on the sides of my face.

"I need you *so bad*," he huffs, thrusting himself inside me.

I lose myself to him, feeling full, and wanted. Grabbing his biceps, I close my eyes and stay in the moment. *Remember this moment, this feeling.* His speed increases, his hot breath on my face, and I bask in the full-body heat. He moans, and I reach down to his hips, pulling him closer, holding him as close as I can. He kisses my neck and I surrender to the incoming waves of pleasure as they crash over me.

And for just a little while longer, I'm not alone. I'm not scared.

For a little while, nothing matters at all.

10

My heels click against the tile floors, echoing in the front foyer of the high school. Sneakers squeak to my left, and Kellan jogs around the corner in her athleisure wear.

"Chels, hey!" She stops and shoves her clipboard under one arm and the basketball under the other. "What are you doing here on the weekend? It is the weekend…isn't it?"

I can't tell her what I'm up to. She'll try to talk me out of it. She's the responsible one, trying to keep me on track, but I can't let her this time.

"I just had to see Meghan."

"Oh." She glances down at the envelope in my hand. "Everything okay?"

I try to come up with something, but she's already walking backwards, toward the gym.

I nod. "You headed to practice?"

"Yeah. Can't be late." She presses her lips together, as

if still evaluating the need for a deeper conversation. "Call me later?"

I nod and as she starts to turn around, she stops in front of the glass display case with the framed photograph of one of our former students. Her name, Shay-Lynn, is etched into the gold plate below. Fencing medals surround the frame from her time competing in regional tournaments.

Kellan reaches out and touches the glass, turning to me with a subdued expression, shaking her head. "This time last year I was writing her university reference letters. I never got to send them, but she would have received grants. She could have..." Her hand falls away as she studies her photo again.

"I can't believe it's been a year," I reply, and rest my hand on Kellan's shoulder.

Shay-Lynn went missing last fall. Her car was found over twenty miles from her house, two cities over. Everyone who knew her knows something terrible must have happened. She was talented, smart, and responsible. She'd never have abandoned her family, her friends, and the bright future she had ahead.

"I think about her a lot," she says, before clearing her throat. "I keep waiting for her to show up."

Most of us have resigned ourselves to the fact that we won't see Shay-Lynn again, but Kellan's hope reminds me of the bond they shared; mentor, and mentee. It happened around the time of the fourth memorial, and I wasn't in the right headspace to support her. I haven't been there for her like she has for me. The pain on her face brings the guilt I carry to the surface again as she side-steps away, checking her clipboard. I wish there was some sort of comfort I could give her.

"Hey, I'm sorry. I know she really looked up to you—" I start, but she bows her head and turns away.

"Call me," she says over her shoulder, and jogs toward the gym.

I slip into the front office.

The reception desk is empty, and I bypass it to the principal's office, clutching the envelope. I squint at Meghan's shadow as she stands from her seat, her back facing the giant window behind her with sunlight pouring in.

"Chelsea, good morning." She folds her hands in front of her. "Is everything alright? Can't remember the last time I saw you here on a weekend."

"May I sit down?" I gesture to the chair across from her oak desk and she nods. "Thank you."

She cares about this school—truly loves it—and whatever goodwill she's felt toward me will vanish once she knows the truth. It will bring unwanted attention, questions from students and parents, and detract from the pristine reputation she's worked hard to build over the three years she's held the position.

Before that, she taught with me. We started here together, almost a year after the murders, when I was finally ready to work again.

"Chelsea, what's that?" She looks down at my envelope.

Once I hand it over, that's it. The first domino. Can I really do it? The alternative would be worse. This way, I get the chance to end things properly, tell the truth, and accept my fate. It's all within my control.

I place the envelope on the desk between us. "I'm resigning, effective immediately."

"What?" She cranes her neck back to study me as I press my fingers to my lips and stare at the letter.

Deep breaths, Chelsea. You're doing the right thing for once, after all this time. But tears pool in my eyes as I stare at the envelope.

"It's all in there. How grateful I am for the position and for all the... grace you've shown me during the difficult times I've been through when I didn't give you the grace you deserved. I've let you down so many times, and you've covered for me—"

"Chelsea, if this is about the missed time, I told you, I understand." She rests her hands on her hips. "We all do."

I stare out the window to the tree just outside her office. The bare branches provide no shade. It's dead—been dead for at least a year—but they haven't gotten rid of it yet. Some things linger far past their time, no benefit to anyone, all because no one's put an end to it.

"I'm doing the right thing, Meghan. It's what I feel is right."

"Do you know what that means?" She nods at the letter. "That's official, Chelsea. I can't take it back once I've notified the board. This isn't like last time."

The last time I found myself in the office after a week's worth of disappearance, stuck in bed, unable to face the days, she gave me a warning. If I needed time off, all I had to do was book it—even on short notice—not showing up for class was negligent, irresponsible, and she couldn't let it happen again.

I was offended, though I knew she was right.

I'm a flaky teacher, a cold fiancée, an absent friend, and despite it all, they make allowances for me because of what I've been through and because of who they think I am. A survivor. A hero. Wait until they finally see what I see. I have to put as much distance between us as possible to soften the blow.

"I understand this is final," I say.

"Chelsea, the students look up to you so much. So many of them got close to you last year, after Shay-Lynn's disappearance. Oz is great, and they've learned to trust him, but he was new back then. When they needed someone to talk to, they went to you. Your absences are nothing compared to the *presence* you've given them. Do you realize that? I think they felt you understood them on a different level, after what you've been through. Their grief was lessened because of you."

I blink up at the ceiling, hoping to keep my tears at bay as the frightened voices of the students echo in my mind from those months.

"The students—think of them. They think so highly of you."

I take a deep breath and do my best to shut the thought out, rising to my feet. "You've been good to me, Meghan. Better than I ever deserved. I'm sorry to leave like this, but I have to. I don't expect you to understand right now. I just wanted to thank you in person for everything you've done."

She shakes her head. "You have nothing to be sorry for, Chelsea. You apologize too much. We'll miss you here."

I walk out of the office and close my eyes, navigating the foyer to the double front doors by memory as her words sink in. My heart pounds in my ears. They'll be sorry they trusted me—and by the time they know the truth—no one will miss me at all.

"Chels?" Oz's gravelly, medium timbre stops me before the first set of front doors. I open my eyes and turn to him. He's leaning against the doorknob to his office, studying me. "What are you doing here?"

I didn't want to see him. Not after yesterday, when he no-showed the memorial.

"I just had to drop something off."

He nods and runs his hand through his dark, curly hair, so casually. Isn't he going to mention it? Apologize? Did he forget?

"Everything okay?" he asks.

If this is the last time I see him, I have nothing to lose. I might as well find out why he didn't make it.

I take a deep breath. "You didn't come yesterday."

His chest puffs out and he shuffles his weight from one foot to the other. "I figured you'd want to just be with the people you're closest with."

I open my eyes wide in objection but press my lips together. He notices and avoids my stare. I told him about what I've been through for the first time last week, when a few of us went out for drinks after parent-teacher conferences. We were the last to leave the rooftop patio, and he sensed my tension. I told him about the upcoming anniversary.

He confessed he knew a bit about my past, and reassured me that I didn't need to share anything I wasn't comfortable with. He's one of the few to ever say that to me and mean it. I didn't share anything more and he didn't ask, but he told me he'd try to make it as a show of support—if I wanted.

In a vulnerable moment, I told him I did. I don't know what I was thinking—I don't usually want anyone around me that day—but I let him know he's an exception, and beyond some attraction to him, I wasn't sure why. I feel I can be myself with him. I've never felt nervous around him because of it. I wasn't forced to lie about anything. He didn't try to tell me how brave I was for what I went through, or how sorry he was for it, either. Just that he was there. Buddhists say the greatest thing you can offer another is your presence, and I wanted to feel his. I thought he wanted mine, too. I was wrong. That makes this easier, but it doesn't feel any better. Better he hears the truth from me.

"I quit, just now."

He blinks quickly at me as if I've smacked him across the face—his eyes are wider than mine when I reacted to his excuse. He doesn't bother to hide it, either. He rubs his fingers over his short, scruffy beard without breaking eye contact.

"Going to play guidance counsellor with me? Try to convince me not to make a big, permanent decision during a highly emotional period of stress?" I release a light huff of laughter to break the silence.

He shakes his head slowly. "No."

I'd know what he would've said, had I not assumed. I won't know what would have become of our friendship and new connection. I won't know if any of the feelings I feel between us are reciprocated. I've been here before. It's too much like Lennox...

I turn on my heel and push the door open. I walk

through slowly, expecting to hear my name, or something from him—something to make me stop, to prolong the day before the largest confession. Nothing comes.

I get back home, greeted by smells of bacon and maple. I kick off my heels, salivating at the scents permeating the air as my cell phone vibrates. I check the message.

Kellan: *I'm sorry I was in a rush this morning. It's a hard time of year for all of us. I was thinking... how about a girl's weekend? You, me, and the spa?*

She's the best friend I could ever have asked for, yet I'm hiding things from her, too. She supports me with no strings attached. Once she knows the truth...

"Where'd you go this morning?" Cam calls from the kitchen. "The gym? I figured you'd be hungry when you got back. I just got in from mowing the lawn and started..." I enter the kitchen and he stares at me from beneath his blue ball cap, his gaze lingering on my skirt with a surprised expression melting into a grin. "You look nice..."

I can't do this now. Not after he put in all this effort. Not after last night. Not after the way he's looking at me with love in his eyes. Leaving him won't be the hardest part of this for me, which is all the more reason to do it like I planned.

"Cam—"

"You don't have to talk about it." He rounds the counter and wraps me in his arms. My head naturally falls against his chest. "I know yesterday was hard, and like I promised, no more trying to get your brother involved."

I frown and lift my head. "What do you mean?"

"I understand why you just leave it." He gazes down at me. "I won't bring it up again."

"You said trying to get him involved... what did you do, Cam?" I pull away from him and he lets me.

"I messaged him on Facebook and asked him to come and support you yesterday."

I take a step back.

Cam continues, "I told him it would mean so much if he could find it in him to let the past go, let go of any animosity, and just be there for his only family member on the most difficult day for you."

"You went behind my back and contacted him?"

He rounds the counter again, grabbing the tongs and returning to the stove. "I thought I was helping—I was just trying—"

"You didn't get a response, did you?" I cross my arms.

He turns away from me and shakes his head, no, picking at the bacon.

"Cam, I can't do this anymore." I can't keep lying. I can't keep pretending I've moved on in any way. I can't pretend like he betrayed me when I'm a liar, too.

He turns to me, cranes his neck back, and frowns. "What? Chelsea, you can't be serious right now. I'm sorry! I shouldn't have—"

"That's not why."

"I don't understand." He clutches the tongs in his hands absentmindedly, and my heart aches.

"We can't work. For so many reasons, and none of this is your fault. I care about you, Cam. I just can't do it anymore."

"Why? Is it because of yesterday? Are you depressed?"

I press my lips together, shaking my head.

"No." He tosses the tongs into the sink with a loud clatter and rounds the counter to be by my side. "This isn't you."

"You don't know me, Cam. Not really. Not in the ways you deserve to know the woman you're spending your life with. You make me feel like I'm the only person in the room—the only person that really matters. Have I ever made you feel that way?"

His chest heaves as he stares at me, taking his hat off and running his fingers through his hair with an anguished expression. He tosses the hat onto the kitchen table. "Chels."

"I don't love myself, Cam. And therefore, I can't love anyone. You deserve someone who will love you in all the ways you need."

"I *need* you." Tears well in his eyes and he reaches out to me. "You have everything I need to be happy."

I take a small step back, out of his grasp. "The person you see when you look at me—I wish I was like her—or that I could be her for you. I'm not. And I can't."

He shakes his head violently. "Chels, you're not making any sense right now."

"I am to me, and it's scaring you, and I'm sorry. In the long run, you'll be glad. You'll have a real chance to be happy with someone."

His Adam's apple bobs in his throat as his expression melts into something cold—stoic.

I try to take a deep breath, but it's difficult. Too hard to see him like this.

He speaks through his clenched jaw. "You've never truly been happy, have you?"

I shake my head.

He knows. Despite the act I've put on since we met that day at the cafe, he's always known. He thinks if he can love me enough, it could change, now he knows it won't.

"It isn't you, Cam. I'm sorry. I'm really sorry." I grab my purse and he steps toward me as I turn away from him.

If he touches me—tries to hold me—I'll step back into the same pattern we've created. Hero and damsel in distress, like Lennox said, but these aren't the roles we're meant to play. When you try to save a damsel in distress, all you get is a distressed damsel. No one deserves that.

"Chels, you can't. You can't do this—"

"Thank you for everything," I whisper as I walk down the hallway to put my heels on.

"Chelsea!" he calls to me.

I rush outside, but the fresh air doesn't help me breathe. It's not until I get into my car and close the door that the tears come. He'll know the truth soon enough, and he'll understand why he's so much better off without me. He'll feel vindicated. Free. He'll never know about the letter, or that his safety is at risk, as long as I keep my secrets.

I'm selfish. I stayed because he took care of me and it felt like the sun—warm and cozy and vibrant—at the same time, that warmth could leave a burn; like I got too close to something I never deserved, and I paid that price, too.

They paid for what they did. Now it's your turn. Tell the truth, Chelsea, or more will pay.

Today, I confess.

Tomorrow, I'll live my first, full, honest day.

There will be suffering, but it's a means to an end on my own terms.

This is what I have to do to prevent anyone else from getting hurt.

I have to stick to the plan.

11

PAST

The look Ellie gives Steve chills me more than the man himself as he marches through the sand toward Morgan, the row of shadowy trees towering behind him. She's never seen him before, but she knows he's an intruder—that something bad is about to happen.

They have no idea.

Steve stops before Morgan and John, fists clenched at his sides. I push the blanket off my lap and walk around the fire toward him, kicking sand up behind me.

"Are you kidding me, Morgan? You found some guy to fuck already? Who is this?"

I step between them while maintaining eye contact with Steve. "You need to leave. Now."

"Oh, fuck off, Chelsea." He raises his hand and shoos it at me like I'm a bug before turning his attention to Morgan behind me.

I take a step toward him, intercepting his line of sight. John grabs my wrist, but I shake it off. I'm tired of this—the intimidation, the threats. She's always checking her phone, looking over her shoulder, and Steve gets off on it. Men like Steve love power and dominance.

"If you come near her again—" I sneer at him, staring a hole through him. I hope it burns.

"You'll what?" Steve laughs and puffs his chest out. "Call your brother? Gonna get big bro to handle things, like always?" He looks over me at Morgan. "He doesn't know how you moved on so soon, either. Doesn't make sense. I did everything for you. Everything you've ever wanted, I got you. I built my life around you—and this is how you treat me?" He points at John and laughs. "This is embarrassing, dude. You like my sloppy seconds, huh? Really enjoying that?"

John steps forward as I try to position myself between them. Steve's falling back—no—he's being dragged.

Austin yanks him by the back of his shirt until Steve trips over himself through the sand, falling on it several feet away from us. Austin turns back around and walks to the front of him, pointing down at him. "You're getting back in your car and you're leaving, man. You're not wanted here, nobody has the patience to tell you twice, and you don't want to make me show you."

Steve stares up at him with red cheeks, glowing by the diluted light of the flames. He scrambles to his feet and looks past Austin to me, and then at Morgan. He points at John. "You better watch—"

Austin grabs Steve's wrist and twists it behind Steve's back until he hollers out into the night. He leads him back toward the trees in the same position until Steve shakes him loose by stumbling, almost falling. Austin lets him go. Steve doesn't turn around as he stomps through the trees, disappearing. Austin stops within sight, seeming to stare after him.

I feel a hand on my back and turn around. Morgan's in tears, and I pull her into a hug.

"If I'm such *a slut*," she sobs, "if I'm *sloppy seconds*, why won't he just leave me alone?" she chokes out.

I rub her back and look up as Lennox and Ellie stand side by side, watching with matching sad expressions. They've never looked more like twins.

Morgan pulls away and wipes her eyes, sniffling and shaking her head. John looks at me and I nod to him, taking a step back. He rubs her arm and leans in, whispering something to her. I turn around and Austin's walking back toward us—stumbling.

"You hurt?" I call.

Steve didn't get a chance to touch him. I know that couldn't be it. Austin shakes his head and John approaches him, pulling him into a hug.

"Man, that was perfect timing," John says.

Austin claps him on the back a few times.

"You gotta be kidding me." There's an edge to John's voice as he pulls away.

Austin stares at him with confusion. "What?"

John walks back toward us, shaking his head, mumbling, "I can smell it on his breath. He's drunk. He's drunk, and you drove here, didn't you?"

Austin's expression melts into something more somber, his eyes lacking focus, and it hits me, too, seconds after.

John stomps toward me but he's looking past us all, out at the water. He turns quickly and shouts, "Do you *want* to die like Murray did? You want to kill other people while you're at it? Huh?"

"Man, hey, listen," Austin calls as he walks toward us.

If he's trying to walk a straight line, he's failing, even on solid ground before he reaches the sand.

"No, this is fucked up!" John shouts, pointing at him. "How can you do this? You want to put me through it all over again?"

"It wasn't just you!" Austin shouts, kicking up sand behind him. "He was my brother, too."

"He was *my brother*." John beats his chest twice. "He was your best friend. What are you doing?" John rakes his fingers through his short hair as he turns away from him toward the water again, shaking his head.

I exchange a look with Morgan, but her glassy eyes are lost as she looks from John to me and back. She must feel as helpless as I do.

"Listen, maybe we should go back to our place," Lennox says, walking through the smoke wafting from the fire on the breeze toward John.

Ellie follows him, her arms folded tightly in front of her, coughing through the smoke.

I turn around and Austin's standing there, before the fire, tears shining in his eyes. He's staring at John as if willing him to turn around. Willing him to forgive him.

"I can't believe this shit," John mutters to Lennox. He shakes his head at me, eyes wide open, seeming to ask what to do.

I don't have enough time to speak before he's looking at Morgan.

"I think we should do what Lennox said." She says to John. "We should go back. I don't want to be out here anymore. He could still be here—watching. I feel safer in the house."

A chill creeps up my neck, and I nod, wrapping one of my arms around her. Maybe a restraining order will work after tonight.

"We should go to the police," I say.

She shakes her head. I knew she wouldn't be up for it, but I had to try.

"It'll make it worse," she says. "I just want to go."

I squeeze Morgan's shoulder. "Let's get you home, okay?"

She opens her mouth, but her breath catches in her throat. "I'm scared, Chels."

"I'll stay the night at your place, okay?"

She nods and I breathe a sigh of relief. She knows she's safe with me. I'll do whatever it takes to make sure of it.

12

As I leave the bank, gray clouds roll across the afternoon sky. My cell phone vibrates in my coat pocket and a sense of dread fills me. I pull it out, stopping at the curb to check.

Cam.

He's probably wondering where I am, and if I'll come back—at least to get my things—but I won't need them where I'm going. My only meaningful possession is now inside the envelope in my purse, and soon, it will be my brother's.

After I confess, there's no way I'll see him again. It gnaws at the pit of my stomach that I'll never get to hug him, be held by him, or my niece and nephew again. I've only ever met Timmy once when he was a baby. He'll never know me. Maybe that's a good thing. It's better this way for them, and that's what matters.

I drive to the eastern outskirts of Newcastle, and park in front of his house—or I think it is. I haven't been here in five years, and my memory is hazy. Did they have a big maple out front the last time? They must have.

I step out of the car. The smell of freshly cut grass fills the air. I stride up their empty driveway and peek around the side of the house. I can't be sure this is theirs. I could peer into the windows but that might arouse suspicion from the neighbours, and I can't risk anyone going into his mailbox before he or Molly does.

The house to the left has perfect lawnmower marks through the lawn and a woman with short gray hair kneels by her garden beneath the front window. It reminds me of Lennox and Ellie's.

"Excuse me?" I call to her and she uses her hand to shield her eyes from the sun, even with the sunglasses she has on. "Do the Thompsons live here?"

She gives me a stern look, or is that because she's squinting? Does she know who I am? Does she know I'm not welcome here?

"Jordan Thompson?" I ask.

She nods. "Who's asking?"

"I'm—just an old friend. Thank you." I walk to the mailbox and take a second glance at the neighbour who's back to gardening before slipping the envelope inside.

I doubt he'll deposit the money at first, but Molly will talk some sense into him. She's so practical, and she's never understood why he couldn't work things out with me. She sends me a birthday card every year and signs it from everyone. Her kindness has meant more to me than she'll ever know. She'll accept the money. The kids could use it, she'll say. The money might mean more to him than the note I included, for all I know, but I've come clean. It's all I can do at this point.

How much time left?

I check my phone, finding a missed text. Maybe Cam again.

Not Cam.

Oz.

My chest fills with nervous energy as I read it.

I don't like how we left things. Meet at Baxter's for dinner tonight?

That's almost an hour away, on the other side of town. I have a more important stop to make, to see the person I owe the most to. I shake my head and toss my phone back into my purse.

I need to see Kellan.

I have to tell her everything.

13

As dusk approaches, the glowing string lights along the side of Kellan's farmhouse in Newcastle's northern boondocks lead me to her backyard. Two acres of property sprawl behind the house, past a line of old oaks at the end of her mowed lawn, fifty feet back.

She purchased it a few years ago, after she was appointed the high school's athletics coordinator. It was the right move; she was already the basketball coach for the boys and girls, the track team coordinator—she ran marathons, so that was only natural—and also found time to coach the fencing team; that's where she connected with Shay-Lynn. Each responsibility afforded her a little raise, though she'd have done it all for free; she's always loved sports.

We played on the high school soccer team together, too, before I quit; Kellan never stopped when things got tough. I guess that's another reason Morgan and I gravitated toward each other. We didn't take school, sports, or ourselves quite as seriously. We lacked conviction.

A bottle of sparkling water sits on the glass patio table in front of Kellan with two wine glasses. She's always insisted on making our non-alcoholic drinks feel fancy, and she never drinks around me. My friendship with Kellan is based on understanding, solidarity, and presence. She'd say it's based on truth, too. In so many senses of the word, we've been vulnerable with each other. I opened up about the abuse Jordan and I dealt with at home. During college, we'd message back and forth about how we wished we'd gone to the same teacher's college. After that, she shared her worst heartbreak, which stopped her dating seriously again. I told her what I could about what happened that night at 306 Waterfront. She told me about her guilt after Shay-Lynn's disappearance, and that she shouldn't have pushed Shay-Lynn so hard in fencing.

She's always been there to listen. She's never judged me.

This will be the last time I feel that acceptance from her. It chokes me up enough to bow my head so she can't see my tears as I approach. I push them away with my fingers.

"Hey," she calls to me, grabbing the sparkling water bottle and cracking it open. A *pfffst* sound follows. There is panic in the pressure, released once enough room is given to an easy calm. That's how I hope my insides feel after confessing it all to Kellan. She won't understand, but she'll be the first to know the truth, and she's the one who deserves it—who's been there the most for me.

There's a blanket on her lap, and one folded over my seat. I move it as I sit across from her.

"So, there's a rumour going around the school that

you're leaving." She frowns and shakes her head as she pours me some water. "I told them it wasn't true, because I'd have been the first to know." She sets my glass in front of me.

"It's true."

"What?" She blinks at me and tilts her head to the side.

I draw a breath, but I can't hold it. I can't hold anything in anymore.

Her expression changes to concern as she studies me. "Chels?" She frowns and sets the bottle down. "What's going on? Is it about yesterday? The memorial?"

I nod, wide-eyed, as a breeze rustles oak leaves in the distance.

"I know you don't like to talk about it, but you know you can tell me *anything*, right?" She leans forward, frowning. "Chels, you're pale."

"I have to tell you what really happened," I whisper. "Nobody knows, but I have to..." I blow out air, trying to hold it in. "I have to come clean, Kellan, and you're the one who's known me the longest, who's still in my life. You've been the most amazing friend to me since..."

Visions of their bloody bodies flash before my eyes.

"I'm here for you, babe," she says. "I'll be here no matter what."

I shake my head. She won't. This is it for our friendship. I tug the wrinkled letter from my purse and unfold it. I extend it to her. She stands and takes it, frowning, sitting back down as she reads it.

"It's a blackmail letter."

She shakes her head, peering over the paper at me

before turning her attention to it once again. "I don't understand."

I swallow at the lump forming in my throat. If I don't do it now, I'll lose the courage. "It started one night at the end of summer, almost two months before they all died."

She puts the paper on the table with a look of concern, and tugs at the blanket to cover her legs, smoothing it across her lap. She has no idea what's coming.

"We were at Lennox and Ellie's; Morgan, John, and me. We were having dinner together. It was my dad's birthday, and there was just this... weird vibe. I felt strange that whole day, and then Steven was calling Morgan, harassing her. This was just after their breakup. There was a knock at the door. No one was there." I'm back in the house, staring past Lennox into the blackness of the night, feeling an odd sense of déjà vu. "We went down to the beach after, and Steven showed up. I guess he followed us there. He saw Morgan and John. They were close. They were kissing. He confronted them." I swell with anger and anxiety, and when I blink, I'm back with Kellan. She stares at me with wide eyes.

"Just breathe, Chels, okay?"

She's been with me during panic attacks. She's familiar with the routine.

I nod, trying to stay with her. Trying not to go back there.

"John's friend Austin showed up, do you remember him?"

She nods.

"John's the one whose brother, Murray, passed from

drinking and driving. Austin was the brother's best friend. Austin shows up, gets in Steven's face, and chases him off—drags him, really—until Steven practically ran away. I'd never seen anybody stand up to him like that before. I'd never seen Steven look scared. Morgan was shaken. I think we all were. He just came out of nowhere."

"Who?"

Steven, running out from the trees.

Austin, pulling him back, away from us. Protecting us.

I blink. "Both of them, really. It was a lot at once, and then, we realized Austin had been drinking, which meant he'd drank and drove there. John was pissed."

"Oh wow, because of his brother? Yeah. I can understand that." Kellan lifts her glass to her lips and takes a small sip, never taking her eyes off me.

"John was hurt that he'd do that—risk his life and everyone else's—after what happened to his brother. I think in the moment, I was too grateful for what Austin did with Steven to be angry with him. He—he protected us. I don't think John would have been as upset if he hadn't been drinking, too. They were like brothers..."

Kellan nods, but she's a blur to me through my tears as I picture the firelight against the twins' faces. The unsettling feeling inside, knowing there would be no going back to how things were before.

I didn't know the worst that night lay ahead.

I can still smell the smoke from the fire.

I can still taste the fear.

I can still hear Ellie screaming.

"John killed him," I sputter, looking up at Kellan. "He killed Austin, and we all just watched it happen."

Kellan stares in horror as I wipe my cheeks.

"I felt like I was dying. I'd had panic attacks before, but never like that. I'd never experienced anything like that night."

"My God, Chelsea... He killed him because he—he was driving drunk? That doesn't... I don't understand."

"That night, Austin admitted he was the one driving the night John's brother died. Murray was drunk and called Austin, asking for a ride. But Austin was drinking too. They crashed, and he fled the scene. He left Murray there, dead. John was in shock, and then he was furious. He told me... he told me he was going to do it." I release a shuddering cry, breaking the quiet atmosphere surrounding the property.

Kellan plants a hand over her mouth, staring at me.

"And we," I choke on my words, but I have to finish. "We covered it up."

Kellan stands and as I cry, staring up at her, I'm sure she's about to tell me to leave. She approaches me and I go to stand, but she bends down and wraps her arms around me.

"I've been living with this for five years, now," I choke out. "I never told anyone."

She rubs my back and I sob in her arms, my whole body shaking. She's so kind. I don't understand. Does she think I'm the victim? She lets go and takes a step back. I study her expression, but I can't read it. I wipe my wet cheeks with the backs of my shaking hands.

"Holy shit," Kellan mutters, stepping away from me. She's in shock. Will the police be, too? Who would expect me to tell the truth after all this time? Only the black-mailer. I push the blanket off my lap, checking the time. If the blackmailer meant for the time to start when I took the letter inside, I don't have long until I have to be at the police department.

"Chelsea... you covered up a *murder*?"

The words give me chills.

She opens her mouth and closes it again, turning back to her seat. She thinks I'm a monster—that we all were. This is what everyone else will know.

"Where..." she hesitates, taking her seat. "Where is the body now? What—what happened after?"

"I don't know where Austin's body is. Nothing happened after—"

Kellan cranes her neck back and frowns. "No one went looking for him? Weren't his family and friends wondering where he was?"

"He'd go on trips all the time. He—he'd go for long periods without seeing anybody. We all thought he was just grieving, but it was the guilt... the shame..."

I remember the look on Austin's face that night. I could see the desperation in his eyes, but I never knew it —never truly knew the weight and pressure his secrets kept him under—until I did the same thing to him.

"Chelsea." Kellan shakes her head, her eyes narrowing. "You've let his loved ones believe he just—left? And they bought it?" She chokes on the last word.

Now she understands what I've done—what I'm capable of.

"I'm turning myself in tonight, Kellan. I'm going to the police right now, before things get worse—before anything else can happen."

Her chin trembles as she studies me, her sadness twisting into a pained expression.

"You know how hard it's been for all of us since Shay-Lynn went missing." She presses her hand to her forehead. "Hell, you counselled half of her grade in the months that followed. You *know* the pain it caused us. I still imagine her coming back—to her family. I know her mom still wonders. We still talk. Austin's family must wonder. How could you... how could you do that to someone? To a family?"

I never thought I could. Until you're in that position, scared and panicked, you don't know what you'll do. I never thought I'd be capable of admitting this to anyone until...

I stare down at the letter on the table and reach for it. Kellan grabs it first and holds it up, reading it again.

"You're right. What we did has damaged so many people. I'm going to confess, and it... it might give some people answers they've been searching for, but the families of my friends will be shattered."

I think about Simon; sitting with him and listening to music. Talking about the twins. Telling me how thankful he was that I was there for Ellie in her final moments. I think about John's parents, still not knowing that the death of their son, Murray, wasn't his fault. I think about Morgan's parents, and how they've been so kind to me, treating me not only as their own, but as a heroine.

When people put their heroes on pedestals, there's a lot of room to fall from grace. If I think about tarnishing my friends in the eyes of their families any longer, I won't be able to do it.

Austin's family will learn the truth. Kellan's right. They've suffered enough—so much—I've never been able to think about it without spiraling into a deep depression.

I rise and hold out my hand for the letter. "I'm ready to take responsibility for what I've done."

"You'll go to prison," Kellan blurts, staring up at me from the paper.

I nod. "I've spoken to a lawyer."

"You'll take the fall, when it was John. Are you ready to do that? Have you—have you even tried to look into who sent this?"

I take a deep breath and look her in the eye. "No. I don't even know if it's real."

"This isn't only a threat to you—it's a threat to the people you love." She hands me the letter and crosses her arms.

I shake my head. "I don't have family anymore, Kellan. I ended it with Cam, and I have *you*. I wanted you to know the truth. I'm going to tell the police. I'm going to stop whoever this is from hurting anyone."

"Chelsea, this is..." She shakes her head in disbelief.

"I know. I'm sorry I lied to you. Thank you for being here for me, Kellan. I'm sorry I didn't get a chance to repay you—to be the friend you deserve—but this is who I really am." I pull my purse strap over my head and across my chest, then take a step back from the table. "I never meant to hurt anybody."

She doesn't respond, and I don't expect her to. I walk across the grass toward the side of the house.

"Chelsea, what are you doing?" she calls.

I turn to her, clutching the strap of my purse. "Going back to where it started," I call. "And then, I'm turning myself in."

She stands by the table in a stupor as I disappear around the corner. I walk down the path, following the string lights out of the yard as light fades from the sky, my legs shaking beneath me.

14

I park beside the curb between streetlights across from Lennox and Ellie's place, and stare up at the front door. I remember Morgan and I heading in for the first time, and how welcoming the twins were. We all just clicked: Lennox, Ellie, Morgan, John, Austin, and me. Our easy connection felt too good to be true from the beginning.

I twist the key and take it out, clutching it in my fist as I turn, looking out the passenger side window at the water. At the well-trod path we took to the fire.

My cell phone rings in my purse, and I dig it out, glancing back up at the house.

Oz's name glows on the screen.

Should I ignore my one last chance to speak to him before it all goes to hell?

I hit the green button and press it to my ear. "Hello."

"Chelsea? What's up? You never got back to me." Several voices chat and laugh in the background.

"Oz, are you at Baxter's?"

"Yeah... are you hungry?" His warm, gravelly voice usually eases some of my tension, but I can't think about anything except what I'm about to do.

I lean back against my seat, sighing. "No, I'm sorry. I won't be coming."

"Oh." He can't hide the disappointment in his voice.

Maybe he isn't trying to. I don't get it. He didn't show at the memorial, but now he wants to see me?

"Oz, why did you ask to see me tonight?"

"I'm sorry if I hurt you when I didn't show up for the memorial. I didn't realize how much it meant to you that I came."

That hurts to hear. Makes me feel like there's nothing he sees in me at all but a sad, lost woman.

"The hurt in your eyes in the hallway," he continues. "That wasn't my intention. Listen, the memorial felt like this thing that I'm not a part of—a piece of your life I don't fit into—and that I just didn't belong there. It was selfish of me—"

"Oz... did you come?"

"When you told me about the memorial the other night, and I saw the pain in your eyes, my intention was to show up for you, and I tried. I went, but I couldn't get out of the car."

He came. I inhale a full breath of relief. Was he parked right here? Did he see me?

"There were all these people I didn't know, and I saw you and your fiancé. You were crying, he was comforting you, and it just didn't feel like I should be there. I didn't know what to do after that. I left. I felt like an asshole."

I shake my head. He shouldn't. It makes sense. He came, and he saw me with the face I put on for everyone, with the man he thinks I've chosen forever with. His vulnerability surprises me. I don't know what to say.

"Then, when you said you quit today, I just didn't want to leave things like that."

"How *do you* want to leave things, Oz?"

I need to know, because this is farewell. He won't talk to me again after tonight when he knows what I've done, and I won't blame him.

"I'm sorry I wasn't there for you."

That's it. That's all this is. This could have been a text, but he's a standup guy, and wanted to say it in person. It's my fault for hoping for something more.

What am I even doing?

"No apology necessary, Oz. You don't owe me anything."

"Wait, Chelsea. Listen, I get the sense that there's something else going on here. Is something going on? Do you need to talk about anything? I wasn't there for you yesterday, but here I am now."

I look at the front bay window of the house and an image of Lennox flashes before me, rising from the dining room table, asking me to dance. I never got an opportunity to tell him how good I felt when I was around him, or how his kindness, passion, and smile were contagious. I never got to tell him how safe he made me feel, or that I was attracted to him. Or that I wanted to kiss him. I never knew how he felt. I was too vulnerable to admit it. It was too much risk. We were too good of friends. I was too scared of rejection changing things between us and a group that had become more like a family.

Maybe it's time to just say how I feel. Maybe this time,

I can make sure there's no regrets, and then I won't have to spend any time wondering.

I take a deep breath. "There's something I wanted to tell you, but I couldn't. Not until now."

"Okay," he says slowly.

"I'm attracted to you. I've always wanted to get to know you better, but because of how I feel around you, I couldn't do that. I was engaged. I couldn't explore—or pursue—I just couldn't go there." I pause, giving him the chance to interject, hoping he will. "Things would never work between us. Definitely not now. Maybe that's part of it, too.... maybe I've known that. Did you know?"

"Okay, Chelsea," he pauses and I wait, holding my breath. "I didn't know any of this."

I nod, my stomach twisting with his words. "How could you have?" I ask playfully, trying to mask the stinging absence of his reciprocation. Why do I do that? Why do I care? Why does it matter anymore? "I thought whatever I felt between us—I thought you felt it, too."

I'd have said the same words to Lennox, hoping he felt it.

I never got my answer with him. I have my answer with Oz. It was just me.

If Lennox had done the same, what would have happened? Rejection would be hard, reshaping the group dynamic would be awkward and terrible and unfulfilling, and nothing would be the same.

But what if Lennox felt the same way?

Every possible outcome was gone, now. This time, I have no regrets.

"I've got to go. Take care, Oz." I twist my key in the ignition and end the call.

Just the truth from here on out. And only one thing left to do.

EACH TURN I make closer to the police department alleviates my anxiety. Almost there. It's almost over.

Is it really? A small voice asks. I'm not sure if it's mine. How could you lie for five years about something like this? How could you pretend you were all victims? You can't just tell the truth to absolve yourself of all the things you did—the *people you hurt*.

Before I realize it, I'm parked in the lot, the glowing glass doors of the police department straight ahead.

I have to do it now, or I won't at all.

I reach for the keys, and realize I have no idea what will happen to my car. I should have asked the lawyer. Maybe Kellan can take it. She can have it.

My cell phone rings in my purse and I reach for it.

The screen glows with my brother's name.

Jordan.

He got the money. He got the note. He knows what I've done.

Emotions churn in my stomach and saliva pools in my mouth. It's all over. I tuck the phone back into my purse and twist the key from the ignition as it stops ringing.

Maybe he'll forgive me one day for what I've done. Maybe I'll even be able to forgive myself once I take responsibility.

My phone buzzes with a notification. An email. Maybe it's from my lawyer.

I'm stalling for time. It's almost over.

I swipe past Jordan's missed call to my email from an unknown sender, an address with numbers. I almost close it until I read the subject line.

You're too late, Chelsea.

I tap the words and a blank email opens with one attachment.

A video. Black, with just a grey chevron to play it.

A terrible feeling boils in my gut as I tap the screen.

15

A close-up frame on something brown and unfocused pulls back into a clear video of a tree trunk in the foreground and a small, glowing fire in the distance. We're all standing around it. John and Lennox are together, Ellie on the side of the fire closest to the water, and Morgan and I round out the circle.

I'm transported back to a time they were alive and my heart skips with the excitement of seeing their faces again before an anxious understanding takes over.

Someone was there, watching us.

Did Steven stay? Did he film this? He was the only other person...

The clip jumps to a different cut. John—lunging toward Austin—his fist raised. It collides with the side of Austin's jaw and he falls back, dropping to the sand.

I squeeze my eyes shut, reliving the shock and horror for a moment before opening them again as the person taking the video gets closer, still concealed in the trees. It comes into focus again as John jumps on top of Austin and hammers on him, punching his face over and over as we watch, stunned. We're in shock, but it appears like we're just letting it happen.

My chest aches and I squeeze the phone in my hand, wishing I could go back to this moment. I wish I'd stopped it right away.

Next clip. I'm by John's side, squeezing his arm in front of Austin's body.

Another cut. A closer shot of me on my knees beside Austin. His blood is on my hands.

Again, closer still. John shouts, "You knew! You knew what I was going to do. I told you I'd kill him."

Now John and I, staring at each other—John, Lennox, and I by the body.

The three of us.

Lifting the body, carrying it away from the light of the fire.

The video stops.

My whole body thrums, shaking with anger and fear.

Someone knows what we did. They twisted it. I look up past my phone at the police department.

Why are they sending this? "I'm here. I'm going to confess!"

I check the time on my phone, but the blackmailer never gave a set time in the letter.

I have to go to the police—to tell them what happened. I open the door and step out, my legs weak beneath me. My phone rings in my hand and I jump.

Jordan.

Maybe he wants to be here for me—even now—when he knows the truth. Hope leaps from my chest to my hand. Maybe I'm not alone.

I press the phone to my ear and answer, stopping beside my front bumper. "Hello."

"Chelsea," his hoarse voice shakes me.

Has he been crying? My chest constricts and I wait in the quiet stillness of the parking lot for him to say something else. Maybe I didn't hear properly.

"Chelsea." A pause follows and I know it's bad. He might tell me never to contact him again. "Molly's dead." His voice breaks at the end.

I freeze. "What?"

"We were driving and some maniac drove us right off the road, and the kids—" No. Please, no. "The kids are okay. But Molly..." He breaks down, sobbing.

I press my hand to my mouth, stifling a cry as his pain rips through me.

You're too late, Chelsea.

This wasn't an accident. This was my blackmailer.

Chills cover my arms as the realization creeps in: They never intended on leaving me or the people I love alone. This isn't blackmail; this is revenge.

"Hello? Ma'am?" A woman's voice speaks.

"Hello, yes," I gasp through my tears, Jordan's crying still audible in the background.

"I'm one of the nurses taking care of Jordan and his children. I used his emergency contact, but they couldn't be reached, so I asked him if there was anyone else he wanted to call. He called you. May I ask who's speaking?"

"This is his sister, Chelsea Thompson." Sister. The word feels foreign. Fake.

"Chelsea, we've got them here at Newcastle Hospital. Jordan is in room one-oh-two, and once you're here, we can let you know where the children are—"

"Oh, I can't—" I stare at the police department, the glowing glass doors waiting for me ahead. I have to tell them what's happening. I have to tell them everything.

I hear the nurses muffled voice before a tapping sound.

"Chels," Jordan says the name he hasn't called me in five years. "I need you. Please. We need you."

I never thought I'd hear those words again.

I rush back to the car and fumble for the keys in my purse. "I'm on my way."

16

PAST

The fire crackles, its smoky scent wafting around us. John stares out at the water with Lennox by his side, showing us their backs. Austin watches him with an anxious expression, the desperation for John to acknowledge him is palpable.

Morgan's breath catches in her throat as she leans in toward me, drawing my attention away from him. "I'm scared, Chels."

"I'll stay at your place tonight, okay?"

She nods and I breathe a sigh of relief. She knows she's safe with me.

"I'm taking her home," I tell them.

"We're all going back." Lennox says.

John shakes his head as Lennox wraps an arm around his shoulders, leading him toward the house.

"I'll put out the fire," Ellie says, and I nod, staying back with her and Morgan as the two men trudge through the sand.

I can't bear to look back at Austin and see the hurt in his eyes, especially after what he just did for us.

"I can't believe it, man," John says, stumbling as he frees himself from Lennox's hold and turns to Austin. "I can't believe you'd do that! Not *you*! You're the last—last person—" He chokes up and Lennox reaches for him again to hold him back.

"Do you have a death wish?" John growls into the night, bending at the waist as if the words have knocked the wind from him.

"Yes!" Austin shouts, stumbling toward us.

"Austin, please," I say, but John's voice drowns out mine before Austin can acknowledge me.

"What the fuck, man?" John shouts, stumbling toward him, evading Lennox's grasp. "You wanna die? You want to leave me?"

Austin covers his mouth and wipes his hands across his face. He wobbles. He's not just drunk. He's wasted.

John grabs Austin's shirt in his fists. "Say it again!" John slurs. "Tell me you want to die! Tell me you want to leave me here without—without the man my brother considered a brother!"

"It should have been me," Austin shouts in his face and John backs off. "I should have died!"

John shakes his head. "No. You can't think like that."

Austin grabs John's shirt in his fists and stares him down.

"Just say you won't do it again," John pleads with him, the anger melted away to a soft quality I recognize again.

"Listen to me," Austin says, stumbling over some rocks by the fire as he backs away from him. "I should have died. I was the one driving. It was me."

John cranes his neck back and we all freeze around the fire. Did I hear him right?

"Holy shit," Lennox mutters, casting a quick glance around the fire.

"What are you talking about?" John shakes his head. "You weren't even there..."

"I was. I was the one driving. Your brother called me at a party, and he was drunk. He asked me to come and pick him up. I'd been drinking, too, but I only had a few. I took a cab there and I figured by the time I got there, I'd be fine."

Dread fills me as the story continues. I can't take my eyes off of him and his anguished expression.

"What ... the fuck ... are you saying, man?" John asks, his words practically electrifying us with his wrath and despair.

"I wasn't paying attention," Austin chokes on his words, breaking into sobs. "We were laughing, and I took my eyes off the road for a second, and I missed the turn. We crashed into the tree and then we... We rolled down the hill."

John glides forward, going face to face with the man his brother considered a brother. "You—you left him?"

"I survived. I don't know how I survived, but I did. The car was on fire. I looked over to my right, and Murray wasn't even there. He—he wasn't wearing a seat belt. He went through the windshield. He was gone."

"Oh my God," Morgan sputters, grasping my arm with her icy hand.

Chills fly across my skin at the vision of a body flying through the broken windshield, flung from the car. My stomach churns and I cover my mouth, trying to quell the sickness.

"You killed him." John says, hardly registering it as a question, yet there's still uncertainty in his voice. He hunches over as though Austin just punched him in the stomach.

He doesn't want to believe it. None of us do. I know Austin's telling the truth. It adds up. It makes sense. He was throwing up in the bushes when we met. His excessive drinking since Murray passed. His long periods of time away from everyone. Not being around enough for John. Seeing what he saw and running. The guilt must have eaten at him, worn him down, until the last few drinks finally opened him up to a confession.

How could he do that? Just abandon Murray...

Austin stares at John, his eyes red, apologetic, defeated. "It was my fault. I killed him."

John runs his hands over his face, unable to recover from bending over, repeating the muttered word, "no."

I go to him, wrap my arm around him, and lead him away from Austin to the heat of the bonfire. I rub his back as he cries, shaking.

"I'm gonna kill him," he says through glistening, tear-soaked hands. I finally see his face. It's swollen with anguish. He looks at me. "I'm gonna kill him, Chels."

The firelight dances on his face as his eyes grow dark. I can only begin to imagine the betrayal he feels as it all sinks in.

"You don't mean that," I whisper, grabbing his arm.

John's sad eyes plead with me, as if somehow I can end the pain. I need to get him away from Austin before things get worse. My heart races as I pull him close. "We're leaving. We're going, okay?"

I look back at the group as they watch us from across the fire with expressions of shock and concern. I have to get John out of here.

17

I step into the doorway of room 102 with little memory of how I got here. I've been mentally preparing to see my brother for the first time in years – it's a diversionary tactic. The video the blackmailer sent is rolling around in my head, too. While I don't know their next move, I know they're somehow responsible for what happened to my brother's family. *I'm* responsible.

A nurse approaches me. "Chelsea?" she asks. I nod. "I'm Heather. Your brother is in the kids' room. I'll take you there."

"Thank you."

I follow her down the hallway toward the elevators, and as we wait for one, she says, "I'm sorry for your loss."

"Thank you," I mutter again.

The same feelings bubble up with her condolences as all the others over the past five years; I don't deserve sympathy—especially not now. Not for Molly. She was a good woman, but I didn't get to know her very well. She made Jordan happy. She was his wife, his best friend, and on top of that, an amazing mother. She was everything to him. I'm the reason she's gone.

Maybe if I'd gone to the police straight away…

"The kids may be transferred to the children's hospital. Your brother should be discharged tomorrow, but timing could be an issue, so it's great you're here."

We ride the elevator to the next floor, and she guides me down a hallway and stops in the doorway of room two-twenty-two. "Visiting hours don't apply tonight," Heather says in a soft voice. "You take the time you need."

I glance into the room.

Jordan sits in a chair in the corner. His head is down. He looks up at me right away.

I start to step inside but he stands and limps to the door, past the ends of two hospital beds, so I stop. Seeing him like this makes my chest ache. As he gets closer, I'm not sure what to expect or what to do. I'm frozen. He reaches his arms out to me and drapes them over me, sobbing into the crook of my neck. It's been so long since I've been this close to him—or seen him this vulnerable —and I squeeze him tight to let him know I'm here for him.

The last time I saw him, I was the one crying.

I'd been invited for Molly's birthday dinner. I had a feeling they invited me to balance things out. There weren't other options from our side of the family, and Jordan was still hazy on the details of the night my friends were murdered and Steven was killed. We'd barely spoken about it, but that night, after most of Molly's family had left, we went out onto the back deck and sat by the fire.

He asked about that night. I didn't want to talk about

it. I'd already rehashed it several times to the police and then each of my friend's families by then. Each time, I had to conceal the reason we'd all gathered that night, and the stress we'd already been under when Steven arrived. I wasn't ready to rehash it again.

Jordan didn't believe Steven did it. I was so taken aback, I started to explain what I'd seen—what I knew to be true. The bloody knife in his hand as he emerged from the room where Morgan and John lay dead. How he chased me with it. I was his one last loose end to tie up. Jordan still didn't believe me, and with that intense, frustrating feeling percolating as he invalidated my experience, I cried, begging him to believe me, furious that he wouldn't.

He asked me to leave.

I couldn't understand how he'd believe his friend over his sister.

The worst part was that he knew something didn't add up. He knew I was hiding something. He knew I was lying to him.

He was right.

Our walls went up that night against each other, and I thought they'd never come down.

Standing in his arms feels like home again.

"What am I gonna do, Chels?" Jordan gasps between his cries.

I run my fingers through his thick hair before pulling away slightly until he's looking in my eyes. "You're going to be there for your children," I say.

He rests his head against my shoulder again as he cries.

"You're going to take this day by day, hour by hour,

minute by minute. Whatever it takes." My eyes dart to and fro along the hospital room floor.

"I—" he gasps, lifting his head. "I—" he shakes his head, his red eyes wide as he gasps for air—for the words. "I can't believe she's gone."

I grab both sides of his shoulders and give them a gentle squeeze until he looks at me, refocusing again. "Are you on anything right now?"

"No. Nothing." He answers clearly, and I see a path through this minute. I need him to focus on the things he knows. "Bella and Timmy. How are they?"

He wipes his eyes and glances back toward the room. "Bella doesn't need to be here overnight, but the nurses want her monitored. She has some scratches and bruises, nothing broken. No real injuries. Timmy... he... the impact from the seatbelt fractured a rib." His voice quavers at the end as he stares into the room. I notice a rough patch of scabbed skin running across the left side of his forehead. "They said he was lucky he didn't tear or puncture anything. They have more tests to run on him, and he might be transferred to the children's hospital, but he'll recover at home with bedrest."

If the sick, twisted person behind the video could do this to my family—to children—they'll stop at nothing to get what they want from me.

If I'd gone to the police sooner, maybe they would have tried to stop me like they did tonight. That's not what they want. They want to hurt me through the people I love.

"They're holding up well. Strong, like their mother," Jordan says.

"And you?" I reach toward his head injury, but he pulls away.

"It's nothing. Just scrapes and bruises."

"And your leg? You're limping."

"It's nothing," he mutters, leaning his palm against the doorframe.

"Can I get you a coffee? Something to eat?"

He shakes his head. "How do we go home without her, Chelsea?" His chin quivers as he maintains eye contact with me.

He needs me right now, but what about when the shock wears off? What about when he regains control of his life and starts to rebuild? Will he still want me around? I'd be there for him in a heartbeat. If he doesn't... maybe that doesn't matter anymore.

"I'm here for you and the kids, and I'm—I'm sorry for not reaching out sooner." The wasted time hits me all at once, with the realization that he could have died, too. I might never have had the chance to talk to my brother again. "I should have called—"

"That." He shakes his head. "That's some petty bull-shit. That was me, needing to be right. I was selfish, and I'm sorry, and I need you, Chelsea. We need you."

It wasn't petty bullshit; I deserved it. I was lying. He wanted the truth, and I couldn't give it to him. I can give him this. I can be there for them. They need me more than I need to tell the truth. I just blew up my whole life, and now, I have nothing... Nothing but family—and it's all I've wanted.

"Let me get a bag with some things for you and the kids, okay?" And take that confession letter and check out of the mailbox. "You message or call with anything you need while I'm on the way, okay, and I'll call when I get there."

He nods, running his fingers through his hair. "Yeah, okay, good."

"The kids favourite stuffed animals, or a blanket, or just—" I don't know what's meaningful to them. I don't know them anymore, but this is the first time I've felt I'll have a chance to.

"I'll send you a list. Thank you, Chelsea."

I shake my head. "Anything you need, okay?" He nods and I walk backwards. "I'm going to bring coffee when I come back, too. One milk, one sugar?"

He nods. "You remembered. Thank you."

"I'll be back in a bit."

He sighs loudly, nodding as he limps a few steps back into the room and I wince, the thought of him and the kids in pain—of Molly—sends anger coursing through my veins. If the blackmailer wants me outed, fine, but not without a fight. Kellan was right. I need to try to find them—find out who's doing this. I have to stop them, somehow

"Jordan?" I call. He turns around and I take a few steps to close the distance between us. "What happened? You don't have to tell me if you're not ready..."

He runs his fingers through his hair and takes a deep breath. "We got rear-ended on one of the concessions a few minutes from Molly's parents." His unfocused gaze falls to the floor. "They ran us right off the road. I didn't get a chance to see anything. The police are looking for who did it. I couldn't remember much... but, Chels, telling her parents was..." He shakes his head and tears slip down his cheeks.

"When did it happen?"

"An hour ago?" he says, still not looking at me. "Maybe two? I don't know. I can't do this right now. It was hard enough with the police. I have to stay good for the kids."

I clutch my purse strap across my chest. "I get it. We'll talk when I get back, okay? Whatever you want to talk about."

He nods and limps back to the corner chair. I stride down the hallway in the opposite direction.

Jordan might not be able to talk about it now, but if the police are looking into it, maybe they'll keep him up to date on leads. Maybe a witness will come forward. Someone driving, or someone who lives along the road.

Steven was the only other person there that night. Could he have taken the video and sent it to someone? I don't understand. Whoever filmed this had five years to deliver it to the police.

Why now?

This is about him. I have to look into his family, and his friends. Anyone who'd want revenge.

I push through the doors of the hospital, out to the parking garage.

Okay, Chelsea. Get it together. You tore your life apart, and now you have to put it all back together to protect your family.

Whoever hurt them won't get away with it.

18

PAST

"All this time," John sputters, keeping his eyes near my shoes. "He lied to me. He lied and made my brother out to be a jackass who died making another bad decision. He was—he was trying to do the right thing."

I grip his arms, my face slightly beneath his, and I stare up at him until he looks back down at me. "I'm sorry, John. I'm so sorry for what happened."

He shakes his head and steps away, out of my grip, rubbing his hands over his face again.

"Chels," Morgan calls, and I turn to her.

Her eyes grow wide in horror as something moves beside me. John—lunging toward Austin—his fist ready to strike. My heart races. Dread washes over me as John's fist collides with the side of Austin's jaw. Austin reels from the hit, landing in the sand with a soft thud. John hops on top of him and wails on him, punching his face over and over.

"Stop!" Morgan cries.

A soft cracking follows. Did Austin's jaw break?

Lennox scrambles to grab John's shirt and tries to pull him off, but he's too strong. I shake free of my stupor, rushing to John's other side, grabbing one of his arms. He rips me away easily, but Lennox grabs the other, and once I have his shirt, we pull together. John stumbles away from Austin, revealing beneath him Austin's bloody nose, fat lip, and vacant eyes. He's looking up at the night sky, unblinking.

Ellie screams, a shrill, high-pitched tear through the quiet night.

"John," I squeeze his arm as he struggles mightily to free himself from our grips. I'm not sure if it's my touch or tone that settles him, but he calms. We let him go as we all stare at Austin, unmoving.

"Holy shit," Lennox mutters, stumbling back from John. Ellie's body stops him. He wraps his arm around Ellie and pulls her face to his chest. He doesn't want her to see this.

"I'm calling an ambulance," Morgan says, walking backward toward the house.

"Morgan," Lennox calls to her, and she stops. "He's already gone."

John takes a knee, eyes locked on what he's done, sputtering, "He—he killed my brother." Only then does he look pleadingly to Ellie and Lennox. "He killed Murray."

I take a step toward Austin, and I think someone calls my name, but I can't hear them through a fresh ringing in my ears. I'm cold at the sight of Austin—of his dead body. Blood is pooling in the sand beneath his head. It must have hit something. The crack we heard...

I fall to my knees, spraying sand on his chest, and

reach for Austin. I press my fingers against his wrist, then his carotid artery, trying for a pulse. I watch his chest for movement.

"I can't—I don't feel anything..." I reach up toward his head—his bleeding head.

Lennox pulls me back. Blood from Austin's hair chills my fingertips.

"He hit his head on a rock," Lennox tells me, and pulls me up.

Now I see the stone, glossy and black by the firelight.

"We have to call for help," Ellie stammers, scanning the moonlit shore. "He could—he could still be alive."

"He's gone." Lennox says, wrapping his other arm around me as I shiver, staring at the blood on my fingers. "We can't help him now."

"We have to help John." I look up as Morgan speaks. Her voice is strong, but I catch the fear in her tone. I wonder if anyone else can—if anyone but her best friend might notice.

"Help... John?" Ellie asks from the other side of Lennox, looking to her brother with confusion.

"Oh, God," John stands, then folds in half, his hands on his shaking knees. He vomits beside the body. Some of the chunks splatter onto Austin's shoes.

Morgan pulls him away, rubbing his back, and catches my gaze.

What do we do? She asks me.

We.

We have to do something. We're in this together.

"We'll tell them what Austin confessed to," I tell her, breaking away from Lennox and Ellie. "We tell them he's responsible for Murray's death."

"Tell who?" Morgan asks. "The police? Chels, we can't. We can't call them."

"Why?" Ellie steps back from Lennox.

Morgan gestures to John. "He didn't mean to do it. We all saw what happened. This was an accident. It was an accident."

But he said he would. He said he'd kill him. I should have done more to stop him.

"All the more reason to tell the police," Ellie says, turning to Lennox, "*now.*"

Morgan shakes her head at me with pressed lips. She likes John, but she's so invested in protecting him, just as much as I am—maybe more. I don't understand...

John wipes his mouth with his sleeve and nods to Lennox. "We hide the body."

They exchange a meaningful stare as Ellie starts toward the tree line, a shortcut to the road.

"Ellie," Lennox calls, and she looks back, exasperated. "We can't. John will go down for this. We can't let that happen."

"What?" Ellie hisses and turns to me. "It was an accident." She's asking me, and I nod, but I'm not sure it was. "That's what we tell them! We don't move him. They'll see the rock. This was never John's intention."

"This wasn't an accident." John takes a few steps toward me, jabbing his finger in my direction. "You knew. You knew what I was going to do. I told you I'd kill him."

"That's enough." Lennox steps between us, holding his hand up to John, and scanning up and down the empty lakeshore. "We're not turning on one another."

Ellie shakes her head. "I'm not doing this. We tell the police."

John shoots Lennox a wide-eyed stare.

"I know," Lennox mutters, waving him off. He calls to Ellie. "All the marks on Austin's face will be reasonable doubt for a judge or jury to think it could have been on purpose—even premeditated. We can't let it happen."

"It *was* an accident!" Ellie shouts at John. "You're not a violent person. We'll tell them what Austin said."

Lennox and John exchange another look and Lennox clears his throat. "You have to tell them."

John runs his fingers through his hair and releases a frustrated groan. "I got called to a bar one time to drive Murray home. He was drunk and belligerent. I got there and he was in a fight. I tried to break it up but the other guy started hammering me and I—I knocked him out, okay? He had to go to the hospital. Murray and I got arrested. We served probation. This could look like I have a history of violence."

"You knew about it." Ellie turns on me. "Did you?"

"No! I had no idea." I shoot a hesitant glance at John but he's not looking at me. "Tell her."

Lennox steps between us. "We're a family. We protect each other."

Ellie storms over, grabs Lennox's hand, and pulls him aside. "I'm your family," she says as they walk toward the tree line. The rest is carried away on the wind.

"Lennox is right." Morgan folds her arms over her chest. "We have to protect him."

John and I don't speak, but we stare at each other. His eyes, glossy and unfocused—unhinged—scare me. I know what he wants me to do—that he somehow blames *me* for this—but I can't go along with their plan. John's chest heaves as he looks down at Morgan. In the firelight, there's still no colour in his face.

"I'll help you," she says, taking an uneasy step toward the body, tripping over a rock in the sand.

John catches her. They grip each other's arms, staring at the body in silence.

They're both drunk. They're not in any condition to make decisions.

Ellie and Lennox return, looking between Austin and the rest of us, waiting for someone to say something to stop this from going further.

"I can't." I choke out the words in a small, quiet voice, turning to John. "We can't."

John shakes his head. "This is your fault, too. You'll go down for this with me if you don't help us."

I open my mouth, stunned, trying to decide what to say—how to challenge him—as Ellie darts down the empty beach. Lennox starts after her.

"Lennox," John says, "you've gotta stay here. I need you. Morgan, you go. Stop her."

Morgan nods, letting go of him, and gives chase down the beach.

I want to run after them, too, but I'm scared of John. I've never seen him like this. I wish I had the answers. I don't. Instead, I stare at Austin's lifeless body glowing by firelight. I stare at him, and I gasp for breath until Lennox's body warms my side, shielding me from the wind and John's gaze.

"Chels?" his voice is kind and patient as I stare at Austin in shock. "Take deep breaths. Go back to the house with Morgan. Make sure Ellie is okay." He squeezes my arm and when I turn to him, I read his expression.

Make sure Ellie doesn't call the police.

Would I want them to do this for me? Is this what you do for someone you love?

Lennox squeezes my arm once more.

"No." John takes a step toward me. "She stays. We need help with the body. We have to do this now. Someone could come walking along at any minute..."

My heart pounds in my ears over the rest of his words.

Yes. Someone. Anyone. Why hasn't anyone come along?

If someone sees, they'll have no choice. It's not too late.

I look up and down the beach. There's no one coming. No one to stop this.

Lennox bends and grabs Austin's hands.

My whole body thrums. It feels like I'm going to die— I can't speak. If I do, I'll swallow my tongue. What a weird thought, but it's with me all of a sudden, and I can't think of anything else.

John grabs Austin's feet and they shuffle through the sand, away from the light of the fire.

"Chels, come on," John calls.

I open my mouth to speak and close it quickly again. I've never felt like this before, I'm sure I'll swallow my tongue. I press it to the roof of my mouth, following them into the shadows, my legs wobbling beneath me. I glance back at the blood-spattered rock where our friend died.

I'm going to die on this beach with Austin.

I'm going to die.

19

The windshield wipers squeak in a slow rhythm, clearing rain from the glass as I pull into Kellan's driveway. I called her after I left the hospital to pick up the necessities for Jordan and the kids, when I realized I had no place to go. I told her about the accident, and she told me to come over as soon as I was able.

I went back to the hospital with the things Jordan asked for and a few others I thought the kids might like. He was sleeping beside Bella when I got there. He faced toward Timmy, fast asleep in the adjacent bed. All I could think was that they lost a mom and a wife because of me.

I pull up the hood on my raincoat and grab my purse, hustling across the driveway and up the porch steps to her door.

Kellan is waiting in the open doorway. She waves me inside, closing the door behind me. Her arms wrap around me. "Chels, I'm so sorry about your sister-in-law."

I hug her back quickly and let go. I need support. It's

part of why I came. I also need her help. I need to tell her everything.

"I made us some tea." She takes a few steps down her long hallway toward the kitchen, stopping as she realizes I haven't moved. "Chelsea?" She frowns, staring at me.

"This is my fault," I choke out.

"What do you mean?" she asks, taking a few steps back toward me. "Wasn't it an accident?"

I grab my phone from my purse, clutching it in my shaky hand, studying her confused expression.

Anyone who sees this video will think the worst of me —that's how it was designed. I've had nightmares about what happened to Austin. I've lived these years riddled with guilt, knowing I could have done more. Knowing it didn't have to be this way. But in my wildest dreams, it never played out the way this video makes it out to have happened.

I tap the email and hold the phone out to her. "The blackmailer sent me a video."

I've told her everything, and she hasn't called the police. She's still willing to see me. Maybe she'll believe me.

She frowns but takes another step toward me. "Of what?"

"Someone was there that night Austin died. Maybe that's who's doing this or maybe it was Steven, and he sent it to someone. Whoever did it—they made it look like I knew John was going to kill Austin—as if it was premeditated."

"But it wasn't..." she waits for confirmation as I keep my hand out with the phone.

"No, but it wasn't an accident, either. Austin confessed to driving when Murray died just before. We all found out at the same time, and I was trying to calm John down, and he said he was going to kill him. I tried..."

Kellan takes the phone and taps the screen. I watch her face, glowing by the light of the screen, as the video plays. Her eyes grow wide and I brace myself for her judgment. The stress builds inside my chest as I prepare to explain anything she questions, hoping she knows me well enough to believe me. I need someone to believe me.

She clasps her hand over her mouth as she watches on, never taking her eyes off the screen.

"You knew!" John's voice shouts. "You knew what I was going to do. I told you I'd kill him."

I wince at the reminder of betrayal. In the moments after Austin's death, I held myself responsible because I trusted John—the man I thought he was. I never thought he'd actually kill his best friend. I thought he cared about me—would protect me the way I was ready to protect him. I thought he was brave after all he'd gone through, but he was so quick to blame me. To shift the blame away from himself.

When I think back on everything that happened after Austin passed, I know John wasn't sorry for what he did. It wasn't a drunken mistake. He wanted Austin to die for what he did to his brother, and he found a way to make us complicit. He got what he wanted. A rock helped. I wonder what would have happened if the back of Austin's skull struck soft sand, instead.

"Chels," she says, looking up from the phone with her hand over her mouth. "I don't understand."

"It makes it look like we all just stood there, but I was in shock. John said he'd kill him, but I *never* thought he'd actually do it, and then..." She turns to me, letting her hand fall from her mouth. "He told me I'd go down for it if I didn't help move the body."

"Chels," she mutters, shaking her head.

I swallow at the lump in my throat and fight to ask the question I'm terrified to have answered. "Do you believe me?"

"I believe you didn't mean for anyone to get hurt," she says right away, and I keep still, waiting for her to finish. Waiting for the *but*. "Chelsea, I thought I knew you, but this is all ..."

My chest tightens, the muscles in my stomach constricting in my desperation. I need her to believe me. Believe in me.

"I wish I'd called the police. I should have done it. Ellie wanted to. I should have gone with her." An image of Ellie breaking away from the group and running across the beach forms in my mind like it was yesterday. "I was scared, and I was having a panic attack. It was the first time it ever happened. I felt like I was going to swallow my tongue—I felt like I was going to die—but it's not an excuse. I'm guilty."

I wait for her to agree, but she stands in silence, still clutching my phone.

"I was on my way to confess when I got that video, and then..." Jordan's cries echo in my mind. "I got the call from Jordan. The subject of that email says I was too late. The blackmailer did this, Kellan. They tried to kill my family."

Understanding flashes in her gaze. "Holy shit."

"You were right. You asked if I'd looked into who sent it. I told you I thought they'd stop once I turned myself in. But this is about revenge. Whoever this is, they want to hurt me. They *killed* Molly. They almost killed my whole family."

Kellan looks down at the phone and back up at me. "What are you going to do?"

I pull the blackmail letter from my purse. "I'm going to find the person who sent this." I nod to my phone in her hand. "And that. I'm going to stop them before they can hurt anyone else."

"This person is dangerous, Chels. Do you think you might already know them? Maybe they worked their way into your life and... and waited? All this time?" She frowns, shaking her head. "But why?"

"I don't know. Tomorrow, I'm going back to Cam's. I'm going to see about any doorbell cams or security footage. Maybe my neighbours have video that shows who put the letter in the mailbox. It wasn't stamped. Someone put it there. That's all I have right now."

She nods, handing my phone back to me.

As I take it, she keeps a hold on it, looking me in the eyes. "I'm coming with you."

I shake my head. I don't want to bring her into it, but she doesn't let go of the phone.

"I was ready to give up, Kellan. You saw me. I wanted to turn myself in. Now they're hurting people I care about. I can't let it happen. If I have to go to the police, then that's what I'll do, but I have to be ready for them to see that." I nod to the phone.

"This was clearly edited. They'll see that, they'll also see what the blackmailer wants them to. It'll be their first impression, and they—they don't know you like I do."

"You said you *thought* you knew me, but you don't, do you?"

She presses her lips together and looks down at the phone in our hands. "I know none of that was your choice."

"But it was."

"John killed Austin. He brought you all into it with him. From everything you've told me, you did the best you could, Chels. You've carried it alone for a long time. If you want to go to the police, I'll go with you. If you're scared of what they'll think, or that it might provoke the blackmailer to do something worse, I understand. I'm—I'm someone they might target." She releases the phone and folds her arms over her chest.

She's right.

"I'm sorry you're involved in this." I shove the phone into my purse and walk toward the door. "I shouldn't have come. I can't let you—"

"I want to do this," she says in a firm tone. I turn back to her. "Let me help you."

I take a deep breath as I wrap her in a hug.

I don't deserve a friend like her, and she doesn't deserve one like me for a whole other set of reasons. We're in this together now. It's the most relief and hope I've felt in a long time.

"Tonight, stay here. Have some tea. Get some sleep." She squeezes my arms. "Tomorrow, we find who's doing this."

I nod, drawing in a shuddering sigh as she holds me.

Whoever sent me the letter and video think they have

all the power, but they don't know the lengths I'm ready to go to for the people I love.

Five years ago, I was forced to help bury a body and cover up a murder.

What happens now is my choice.

20

PAST

Candlelight dances on their faces like the fire did that night, nearly two months ago. We're sitting in our usual spots, same as we did earlier that terrible evening. I glance at the empty seat at the head of the table, opposite John. Whenever Austin came, he'd sit there. He'd exchange little looks with John, inside jokes. They'd both be the loudest voices at the table, battling to be heard over each other as they told stories about John's brother, Murray.

John picks up his glass of water as Morgan rubs his shoulder. He doesn't seem appreciative for her efforts, but he doesn't shrug her off, either.

John called me a few days after Austin died. I only answered because I was afraid of what he'd do if I didn't. In a way, I was grateful; I didn't want to see him. When we spoke, he told me he'd used Austin's fingerprint to unlock his cell phone that night. John sent Austin's closest family and friends a text from the phone, claiming that he was off on his next adventure, and that he loved them. He said he destroyed the phone that night, and he promised he wasn't drinking anymore, just like me. It was a short conversation, but it felt like he was trying to make me feel safe, and maintain a connection with me.

I haven't answered any more of his calls, but he and Morgan have kept seeing each other. I don't understand how she's able to do that after what John did to Austin— to me—but she's had an easier time pretending like it didn't happen. We've been drifting, and when we do talk, we don't speak about it at all. It's still difficult to look at John, and all the more difficult to see Morgan fussing over him.

I've been waiting for Austin's family or friends to report him missing. I'm scared I'll see Austin's face on the news, or online, and a band of people organized to search for him. I keep waiting for John to tell us he's been questioned, as one of Austin's closest friends, about his whereabouts.

Ellie barely lifts her gaze from her untouched plate of roasted root vegetables. She's kept to herself and hasn't returned any of my texts. Lennox told me she hasn't been speaking to anyone. Sometimes, she even ignores him. Lennox's skittish glances around the table increase the fluttering in my chest.

Who's going to say it? Who's going to actually talk about why we're here, for the first time since that night?

"I'll be right back." Lennox stands and disappears into the kitchen.

Morgan's phone vibrates in the pitch-black living room, and John turns to her.

"Is it him again?"

Morgan sighs. "Probably."

I shudder at the thought of Steve still harassing her, as if a cold draft has come upon me. Morgan doesn't talk to me about Steve, much. She has John for that, now.

Ellie looks up from her plate, the empathetic look I'm familiar with back in her stare. Music fills the empty space between us. Another of Lennox's favourite acoustic albums. Easy rock this time.

"He's *still* bothering you?" Ellie asks.

"We tried to get a restraining order against him after... that night," I say, and Ellie turns to me, her stony gaze returning. "There wasn't enough evidence of *imminent danger*."

"That's bullshit." Lennox takes his seat again.

"Yep." John stares at Morgan and she twists at the locket of her necklace, avoiding everyone's stare.

It took some convincing, but Morgan and I went to the police the day after the confrontation to file a restraining order on Steve. I was scared to go after what we'd witnessed that night—scared John would find out and think we were going to tell them about what he did. Instead, it was Steve who found out about our visit, some-how. I think he's following her, still. He told her she was being dramatic and making him out to be the bad guy for loving her. I'm disturbed by his vision of love, but according to the police, nothing he's done warrants protection. We couldn't tell the police about the alterca-tion the night before. We couldn't risk them looking into it further, and he hasn't physically approached her since. According to the local detachment, she has no case against him.

"Has he..." Ellie pauses, picking up her fork. "Tried anything again?"

"He showed up at my work," Morgan says.

"What?" I stare daggers at her. "Morgan, you never told me that."

"My boss had to ask him to leave. He didn't put up a fight, and then he was out front, waiting for me when I left. I'm just glad John was there." She smiles at him and he takes her hand.

"I was picking her up that night—maybe a coincidence—maybe not." John kisses the back of Morgan's hand.

My stomach churns at the sight, all my muscles clenching as I struggle with the new reality that after what happened to Austin that night, they grew closer while it's torn the rest of us apart.

"You think Steve knew you'd be there?" Lennox asks John.

Morgan's phone vibrates again.

"Pretty sure he's followed me before, and that he will again." Morgan releases John's hand and turns over her shoulder to the living room.

"You should leave it," John says.

At the same time, I say, "Don't check it."

We freeze in place at the table, the vibration from the phone continuing.

Why didn't she tell me? Why do I feel like this is something I'm no longer included in? But *John* is?

Morgan shakes her head. "I can't take it."

"You need to block him," John says, taking a sip of water.

"No. I can't take the tension. *This*." Morgan gestures around the table.

"Okay." Ellie tucks her hair behind her ear, staring at

the untouched dish before her. "I'll go first. I can't do this anymore."

"Do what?" Morgan asks.

Ellie looks to me. "We never got a choice in this."

Lennox licks his lips and stares at me, too. The tension between them is palpable, and I know they're both looking to me for validation and support. I'm the swing vote. I can't choose a side between them, but I'm relieved that Ellie knows I didn't stay by choice. Lennox must have told her.

"Not true." Morgan stands. "We all had choices that night, and we made them. No one's in a position to point fingers here."

"I can't live like this," Ellie tells me before turning to Lennox. Her eyes are glistening. "I can't keep lying."

"What are you saying?" John asks.

"She wants to go to the police." Morgan folds her arms over her chest. "Don't you?"

Ellie turns to Lennox. "I want us *all* to go."

John rubs his hands over his face, exasperated.

Morgan also appeals to me. "We can't."

She knows the nightmares I've had—the guilt I harbour—but I haven't suggested confessing. I haven't been brave enough.

"You don't have to, then," Ellie says, "But I do. I can't un-see it. I can't sleep. I can't eat. I don't go out anymore. I don't know how you do it." She turns to her brother. "I don't know how you did it in the first place."

"I was trying to protect us—" Lennox starts.

"John," Ellie corrects him and shifts a withering gaze on Morgan—a look I've never seen from her before. "You wanted to protect John. Like Austin protected us from your crazy ex that night."

John uncovers his face, now beet-red, letting his hands drop to the table with a *thunk*. "He killed my brother, Ellie."

"So, it's just fine, then?" Ellie spits back. "What we did is okay? An eye for an eye?"

John shakes his head. "Nothing is fine. None of us are fine. We should have gotten together before now. We should have supported each other through this like we do with everything else."

Ellie covers her mouth, and from behind her fingers, she whispers, "I don't want anything to do with you." The silence that follows fills the room. Even the music does nothing.

Lennox rests a hand on her back, but she shrugs it off, so he stands and walks back toward the kitchen. He spins, opening his mouth to retort as a knock at the front door provides an interlude.

Lennox and Ellie exchange a cold look before he passes me on the way to the door, his spice and cedar scent leaving a comforting wake behind him. The music fills the room again, far too light for the mood, and we wait in silence.

Nothing comes. The eerie feeling of déjà vu courses through me.

I stand, walking toward the alcove to the front foyer, exchanging furrowed expressions with Ellie. Lennox stands in front of the open door, dead centre, staring out into the night.

I fold my arms over my chest, comforting myself in the cold air. "Lennox?" I call. "Who's there?"

He glances back at me. "No one."

Chills crawl up my spine as he closes the door and waves me over, out of view of the dining room as I faintly hear John urge Morgan once again to block Steve's calls.

I walk toward Lennox, and he leans in. "We can't go to the police. It's too late. We have to stick together on this."

We're all in too deep. "How do we help Ellie?"

He shakes his head with a blank expression. "She trusted me, and I failed her. She doesn't trust the decisions I make anymore, but I think she might listen to you."

"Me? Why me?"

"You two have a bond. She knows you tried to stop it. She respects you—how you handle things, and how vulnerable you are. I don't know if it'll work for sure, but we have to stop her." He takes a step around me, shaking his head, still whispering. "Maybe if you talk to her alone? Morgan's making it worse."

I stare at the closed door and frown. "Why would someone knock and leave?"

"Huh?" He asks, turning to me. I look back at the door. "Chels? You think we're doing the right thing, don't you? Protecting John?"

I shake my head. "It's not right."

He nods slowly. "I hate that I did this to her. To us."

"Why did you, then?"

He stares past me to the door as he speaks. "None of us have a ton of family to count on, except Morgan. We've all been let down by the ones who were supposed to love us—put us first, even. I really thought that's who we became to each other. That's what a good family does. We protect each other."

I nod, but the sentiment feels hollow now that we're so disconnected. He squeezes my hand and it lingers before he heads back toward the dining room.

"This is torture," Ellie cries, light reflecting off her wet cheeks as we re-enter the room.

"You could have called the police," Morgan says, standing opposite Ellie across the table. "I didn't restrain you. I didn't even threaten you. You locked yourself in the bathroom, Ellie. You had your phone. You could have turned John in, but you didn't. Why?"

Ellie's chin quivers and she turns to Lennox.

Because she trusted her brother.

"So, it's his fault?" Morgan asks. "You're twins. I get it. There's a special connection, but you're not attached at the hip. You make your own decisions. So why?"

"Morgan—" I start, but she holds a hand up to me and keeps staring at Ellie.

Lennox is right. We have to separate them and de-escalate this.

"I was in shock!" Ellie cries.

"We all were," Morgan shoots back.

"Ellie," I say gently, "can I talk to you in the other room?"

She turns to me, sniffling, but doesn't move.

"Please?" I ask.

Morgan rests her hands on the back of the chair and offers an apologetic stare, as if finally realizing the moment she's in. She'll get nowhere with her line of questioning.

Ellie stands and rounds the table, walking past me toward the hallway. She goes toward the back bedroom.

I give Lennox a look before following her.

I'll do my best.

"I haven't been sleeping, either," I whisper to her.

She stops mid-hallway and turns back to me. "The police came the other day."

"What?"

"People have come looking for him. Two days ago, an officer came, asking if we knew Austin. He asked if we'd ever seen him before. Lennox said no, just like he told the first guy—"

A heavy knock echoes down the hallway from the front door.

"The first guy?" I ask Ellie.

"He said he was a friend of Austin's," she murmurs, looking past me toward the hallway. I follow. We watch Lennox go to answer the door again. "Who was at the door?"

I turn back to her. "What?"

"Just before, when there was a knock."

"No one," I say.

Lennox stops at the door. Morgan and John appear in the alcove.

We all watch as the door opens.

21

Kellan walks back toward my car from my neighbour's front porch. Once she spots me, in the car, parked across the street, she shakes her head. Another no.

I knew there wouldn't be a good chance that any neighbours would have footage of our front door, yet two had video for us to watch and offered it freely. I watched the motion highlights of the next door neighbour's camera from the past week. No one came near the door except myself, Cam, our postman, and a deliveryman who brought flowers the day before the memorial from Meghan and the rest of the high school staff. I greeted him at the door myself, and he didn't go anywhere near the mailbox. The security footage confirmed it.

That was it for mine; Kellan was watching footage from the neighbour's viewpoint across the street, diagonally from Cam's place. The longer she spent there, the more hope I had.

She slides in the car beside me. "Any luck?"

"Nothing. How about yours?"

"Their camera records twenty-four-seven, but over-writes after seventy-two hours. I saw you, Cam, a mail carrier, and a flower delivery. If the blackmailer brought it before then, there was no video for it. Sorry, Chels. Is that everyone?"

I nod. We canvassed anyone with a view of my front door—Cam's front door. I glance over at the white car in the driveway behind his.

"Do you think there's another letter?" Kellan asks. "They might have dropped one off again."

I nod. "I don't know who he has over. I don't want to go back in there, Kellan."

"Do you want me to go and ask for your mail?"

I sigh and shake my head, no, grabbing my purse. "I have to get some of my things, anyhow. I need to go. It needs to be me."

"I'll be here if you need me."

I go to open the door but stop. "Last night, I dreamt about the night they all died. I remembered my last conversation with Ellie. She told me a police officer came to the house, asking about Austin. She said a friend of Austin's came, too, and that Lennox lied about knowing him. Austin must have... must have told someone at some point that he was going to meet up with John and the rest of us. Someone knows we were friends, and they came looking, and..."

"And maybe that's the blackmailer?"

I nod. "I can't think of anyone else. Austin came to see us, and then was never seen or heard from again." I explain how John used his fingerprint to unlock Austin's phone and send a decoy message. Austin had a standard going away message they'd all received countless times. Then, John destroyed the phone.

I sigh. "We don't have any more leads. I need to look into the people who were friends with John and Austin, his family, all the people who might have received that text." I don't know their names. I don't know what they look like.

After what we did to Austin, after lifting his dead body and helping to move it—for it to be buried some-where—I couldn't bear the thought of his family wondering about him and missing him. Any time my mind wandered that way in those months after, I imag-ined their concern spurring them into action. I waited for a missing person's report. I expected to see Austin's face on the news.

The guilt and shame weigh me down as the realiza-tion hits me. I've felt so scared, and ashamed, always focusing on me; on my life, and how I was going to get by, burdened by my secret. It was easier not to think about the people missing Austin, and what we took from them.

"I don't know what Austin's family thinks, but I'm ready to find out."

I can't take responsibility for what I've done if I don't know the extent of the damage I caused. I've disregarded the impact Austin's disappearance has had on his family and friends—turned away from it purposely to protect myself.

Kellan gives me a look.

"What?" I ask.

She shakes her head and presses her lips together. "I was just... thinking about his family. Just thinking his is missing... wondering..."

The shame and guilt twist inside me, and I can't speak, but I turn to her and swallow at the lump in my throat. I take her hand and she squeezes mine.

"You have the power to do the right thing," she whispers. "You know the truth, and that's something you can give them."

I nod and get out of the car, letting the fresh air in my lungs.

I was going to confess for me, but now, it's for them. I won't leave them to wonder, like Shay-Lynn's parents. I know that's what Kellan's thinking about as I walk toward the house. I'll do what's in my control to give them the answers they need.

22

My heart races as I walk past the white car in Cam's driveway, and then his black one. I hope he's not home; that somehow, in spite of the parked vehicles, they've gone out. I drape my purse over my shoulder and stop before the mailbox beside the door.

I open it, reaching my hand around, but my fingers only graze the metal interior. I stand on my toes, peering inside, confirming it's empty. If there was anything there for me, it's inside the house, now. I knock on the door and take a step back, bracing myself for the greeting I'll get from whoever answers.

The door opens. Cam's sister Callie leans against the knob in the threshold. Her hair is in a messy bun, and she's wearing one of Cam's hoodies that I used to wear on lazy Sundays with him. It hits me that I'll never wear it again. I'll never be held in his arms or share another meal with him. I'll never be greeted by his warm smile, asking how my day was, or what I'd like to do that night, which was almost always only to have a quiet evening with him.

I always felt safe with Cam; as the loss hits me all at once, I look up at her with a glassy stare, hoping I don't break.

"Chelsea," she says, averting her gaze and staring past me.

I deserve the cold greeting, but I'll do what I can to finish up here as soon as possible to avoid being reprimanded for hurting Cam. I deserve it, too, all of it, but I have to find Austin's family.

I clear my throat. "Hi, Callie. Is Cam home?"

"He doesn't want to talk to you."

I tuck my hair behind my ear, filled with a sensation of relief. "I can understand that. I came to get my things and collect my mail."

She takes a few steps back, holding the door open for me.

Several boxes greet me in the front foyer. I stop on the mat.

"It's all your stuff." Callie says. "We packed it up for you."

Cam's brother, Connor, shuffles out from the kitchen. He gives me a cold stare behind his thick-framed glasses. He used to give me a big hug whenever he saw me. So did Callie. He blows air from between his tight lips and shakes his head, grabbing the railing to the stairs.

"I hate that I hurt him." I choke out into the silence. "I'm hurting, too—"

"You gonna act like the victim here, Chelsea?" Connor climbs the stairs, staring straight ahead. "You play the role pretty well."

Shame swells in my chest as he disappears into the bedroom. Cam must be in there.

Callie crosses her arms.

"I never wanted to hurt him," I mutter, trying not to choke on my words again.

"I'm sure you didn't," she replies, staring past me at the door. She can't even look at me. She doesn't see me. "You probably weren't thinking much about him at all. If you had been—if you ever really loved him—you wouldn't have done this."

She's not wrong. There's no defense. No excuse.

I bend and grab one of the boxes. I feel her eyes on me, and I hate to ask, but I have to know.

"*Is* there any mail for me?" I ask, standing to face her. "Any letters?"

"I don't know. Check the mailbox."

I start down the hallway toward the kitchen. "I'm just going to check the counter. That's where we put the mail."

I set the box down on the clean, empty counter, and take a deep breath, scanning the kitchen. My chest grows tighter. My entire airway is more constricted here, wound tight by the disappointment, tension, and self-directed anger as I move through this house that was once my home. It's spotless. No papers in sight. I grab the box and walk back down the hallway, past Callie, clumsily trying to work the door with full hands.

"I should have seen it," she says as I struggle. "But I only saw how happy you made my brother. I saw you through his eyes." I open the door and get a few steps outside.

She holds the door open, leaning outside a little. "I've always felt sorry for you and what you went through. It's always about you, isn't it? You should never have accepted his proposal." She disappears into the house, leaving the door ajar.

She can't understand what I'm going through—or why I did this. It must seem cruel from the outside. I'm being blackmailed. The letter came here. Even if the blackmailer knows we've separated, Cam could still be in danger.

I set the box down and pull the door open. "Callie?"

She stops in the hallway and turns back to me.

"Do you think Cam could stay with you or Connor for a while? So he has some support? He'll never ask for it, you know how he is, but I don't think it's good for him to be here right now."

She crosses her arms, staring at me, and I know it's the best I can do for now.

I drop the box by the trunk. Kellan joins me. I lean against the car for support and suck in as much fresh air as I can. My cheeks feel flushed. "There's more boxes. I don't want to go back in there. His brother and sister are over, and I can't face another firing squad, and I don't want to have to see Cam." I pant and rest my hands on my hips, turning to Kellan.

She nods. "I can."

Before I reply, she's striding up the driveway.

Callie was right. I've been selfish, but I cared about Cam a lot. She can't take that from me.

The blackmailer knows me better, though. They know my life is miserable and built on lies. But I love my family, and they need me. I have one great friend left.

Kellan finishes bringing the boxes, and as we load them into my trunk and backseat, I get a text.

Jordan: *Can you come before four? They're transferring us to the children's hospital.*

I show Kellan the text, and she pats my arm.

"You go. I'll track down Austin's family, okay? What's his last name?"

"Cann. Thank you. I'll drop you off on my way."

As we walk to our respective doors, I take one last look at Cam's place.

Staying with him was wrong. Leaving was right. Leaving was also incredibly hard. I regret so many things in my life, but letting him go isn't one of them. He's safer now, even though he's hurting. He'll have the chance at the kind of love he deserves.

My chest aches as I get into my car. My life with Cam is over.

23

Enshrouded in the dim light of underground parking, I grab my purse and the tray with two coffees and two juices. I spare a glance for my boxed-up possessions in the backseat of my car; they wouldn't all fit in the trunk.

I stop at the gift shop before the elevators and spend a small fortune on a stuffed lion and a stuffed camel, bringing them up to the kids' room along with the drinks. Jordan sits between their beds, waiting, and all three of them stop talking and look up at me as I stop by the end of Timmy's bed.

"Chels," Jordan says, looking up at me with a heavy expression.

The kids eyes light up in juxtaposition to his when they see what's in my hands.

"I brought you two something." I hold up the stuffies.

"Aunt Chelsea?" Bella asks.

My chest expands, and I nod. I take her the lion and

wrap my arms around her gently. She does the same to my neck and I choke back tears.

"Timmy, this is your aunt Chelsea." Jordan says from behind me. "She's here to help us out, okay?"

Bella lets me go and focuses on her lion. I shoot Timmy a smile and give the camel one last squeeze before setting it on the bed beside him. "It's nice to meet you, Timmy."

He looks at me with curiousity and says nothing.

"That's yours." I point to the camel, but he continues to stare at me.

"He's on some meds, Chels," Jordan whispers. "He can't really do much right now, but he's comfortable."

I nod awkwardly.

"You should sit with him," Jordan takes a seat on Bella's bed.

I take a deep breath and settle in gently beside him, grabbing the camel again. He stares at it intently.

"Hello, Timmy. I'm mister camel." I contort my voice to sound squeakier, bouncing the animal up and down across my lap, as if he's walking toward him. "Will you be my friend?"

Timmy nods with a smile. I tuck the camel into his hand and he squeezes it with his little fingers.

"What do you say?" Jordan asks.

"Thank you," both the kids chime in, and Bella finishes with "Aunt Chelsea."

"You're welcome." I smile at them.

Jordan stands and nods toward the door. "We're just waiting on some tests for Timmy and then we'll all go to the children's hospital in the city. The doctor discharged Bella, but I want her to stay with me, so she'll come with us. You're doing so good, honey. He's a brave one, isn't he Bella?"

Bella nods, beaming at her brother.

"We'll be right back," Jordan tells them, and I follow him to the door.

He holds up two fingers to the kids, pointing at his eyes and then theirs.

"Yeah, yeah," Bella says as we continue on, stopping just before the doorway to the busy hallway.

"She's so big," I whisper.

He nods. "Thanks for everything you brought last night. Sorry I wasn't awake—"

"Don't be silly."

"Listen, Bella's coming with us for now, but I don't want her staying at the children's hospital the whole time. Do you think, at some point, you could take her home and stay with her?"

"To your house?"

He nods. "Yeah, of course."

Of course he means their home. I was worried he wanted me to bring her to my non-existent home. I exhale a sigh of relief. "Yeah, I can do that."

"Okay, thank you. I really want to be with her when she goes home for the first time, but I have to stay with Timmy."

"I understand."

"Chelsea..." He struggles to find the words, "I'm hoping you could maybe stay with us. Just for a while—at least until Timmy is released—but even after, I'd like you to be there..."

I nod, but he purses his lips and glances back at the kids. "Listen, if you need time to think about it, I understand. You have your own life. A fiancé." He runs his hand over his scruffy chin. "You know, he came to see me a few days ago."

"What?" Cam told me he messaged him on Facebook. "He saw you *in person?*"

He shoves his hands in his pockets and stares at his shoes. "Yeah. He asked me to come to the memorial. To be there to support you. I thought you knew."

"No, I didn't."

Why did Cam lie about it?

Jordan frowns and looks up at me. "You didn't tell him where I live?"

I shake my head, no. How did he find out?

He sighs. "Well, I'm sorry. I just couldn't do it. Didn't feel like the right time for an overdue reunion."

I shake my head again. "Jordan, I never expected you to come."

I also never expected Cam to sneak around and meddle in my personal affairs.

"Well, your fiancé wanted you to have family support, and I'm sorry—"

I press my hands on my hips to stop them from shaking. "He's not my fiancé anymore."

"Oh. I'm sorry to hear that—wait—when did that change?"

"It's not important. I can tell you later, okay?" He nods. "So, he came and asked you to come to the memorial? Did he say anything else? Ask anything else?"

"I wasn't going to let him in at first, but he said he didn't feel like he was enough of a support to you on his own, and that you weren't doing well. He said around the anniversary you struggle, and it would mean a lot if I could hear him out. He really cares." He gives me an apologetic look as soon as he finishes.

That's why Cam was so disgruntled and shocked when Jordan didn't come. He thought he'd pled my case well enough.

"So," Jordan glances back at the kids. "When you've had some time to think—what I mean is—let me know when you decide if you can stay with us for a while."

I nod, staring at them. "There's nowhere else I'd rather be."

But it's not safe. Not until I find out who's doing this and stop them.

He takes a staggered breath in and sighs deeply. "That's a big weight off my mind. I know when it's time for Bella to go home with you, it could be tough, and I just want you to be prepared for that. I can't imagine how she's going to feel, not having her mom to—to give her a bath, tuck her in... kiss her forehead goodnight..." His glassy eyes stare into mine. "How did you do it, Chels? How did you carry on after losing people you cared about?"

I shrug and shake my head, eager to get off the topic. "We've experienced loss before."

"Mom was tough, but that was different, and we're better off without dad. He was never going to get better, and for a long time, he wasn't acting like a father to us. That was just a fact, but your friends—they were like extended family to you. That's what Steve was to me. Molly—she's my soulmate." His voice shakes with the word and he covers his face with his hands as he sobs silently into them. "I wish it was me, Chels," he chokes out.

I rub his back and squeeze his arm with my other hand without saying a word. His shoulders stop shaking and I gently release him, stepping back to give him space.

"She likes to—to have a story read to her. Before bed. They both do."

"I'll read her a story," I whisper. "However many it takes until she falls asleep."

He nods and gives me a tight-lipped smile. "Thank you. Our next-door neighbour, the one with the beautiful gardens, has a spare key for the house. I'll call ahead and let her know you're coming."

She'll tell him I've already been there... how will I explain that?

No. She doesn't know who I am. I said I was just a friend. I guess she might tell him that, eventually, after I pick up the key, but I'll deal with it then.

Jordan rubs his temple and yanks his hand away with a hiss, squinting as he remembers the gash on the side of his head. "I'll give you a call when I think Bella's ready to go home? Keep in touch 'til then?"

"Sure."

His quiet, somber expression makes my chest ache as he stares out into the hallway. His gaze falls to the tile floor as people walk by.

"What is it?" I ask.

"I can't stop thinking... If I'd gone to the memorial, Molly and the kids would have gone to her folks for dinner that night without me, and then we wouldn't have been driving on that road last night..."

"Hey, you can't do that to yourself. This isn't your fault." I squeeze his shoulder. "You can't think about what-ifs."

He frowns and cocks his head to the side. "Don't you?"

I swallow at the lump in my throat. "No. I don't let myself go there, really. I think if you deal with what is—what you've got to work with—you find more productive things to focus on."

And tucking away all the things I felt guilty of—ashamed of—made it easier for me to avoid blame. To deny it, even to myself.

He nods slowly as a doctor picks up a clipboard outside the kids' room. Heather, the nurse, joins his side and gives me a friendly smile.

"Call you later." Jordan says. The doctor joins Jordan, and the two begin discussing test results.

I head back to my car, checking my phone in the elevator in case Kellan has news, but there's only a missed call from Cam. I can't talk to him now—not yet—especially knowing how hard he tried to make things better for me. My emotions are all mixed up. I don't want to add to his pain. Callie said enough.

The parking garage greets me with its usual glum dampness. I slip my cell phone back in my purse, and on the other side of the overhang, clouds roll across the gray afternoon sky. I get into the car and glance over my shoulder at all the boxes. Everything I own, the life I built, fits there. Maybe I can unpack a few things at Jordan's.

I slip the key in the ignition, and as I look up, I'm faced with a white envelope tucked under the windshield wiper. I gasp, gripping the wheel, and turn over each shoulder, watching for any movement.

Did the blackmailer follow me here?

I check that the doors are locked—they are.

Maybe they've been following me the whole time. They have the video footage. They know what happened to Austin. What else could they want from me, except to see me suffer?

Chills crawl up the back of my neck. I scan the surrounding area again. I know I have to collect the letter, but not until I'm absolutely sure I'm safe.

Maybe they want to know where he's buried. If they had that on video, they would have included it. I don't know exactly where John led us that night. I blocked out so much of it, but if I had to bet, I'd say Austin's body is under the sand, between the road and shoreline. I'd guess it's close enough to the place he died that if someone stood there at the bonfire, screaming like Ellie did that night, the sound would reach Austin's makeshift grave.

I slip my keys between my fingers and pull the door handle, sliding out of the car slowly, watching over my shoulder as I round the door and reach for the envelope. I tug it out from beneath the wiper in one swift motion, bringing it into the car, and lock the doors again.

I slip the paper out, holding my breath as I recognize the same typed font with a different message.

THEY PAID *for what they did. Now it's your turn.*
Tell me the truth, Chelsea, or more will pay.
The house. Waterfront Road. Midnight.

·　·　·

I DIG my phone from my purse and call Kellan, panic rising in my chest as I press the phone to my ear.

They want me to go back. They want me to tell the truth.

If I have the chance to come face-to-face with whoever killed Molly—tried to kill my whole family—I won't let them walk away.

24

PAST

"Morgan!" Steve shouts past Lennox. "I know you're in there."

"Hey, man, this isn't okay—" Lennox starts as I march down the hallway, ready to push him out of the doorway if he tries to come in.

"Morgan, I need to talk to you," Steve hollers.

I pass Morgan, standing beside John in the dining room. I mutter, "I'll handle this."

"Tell her I need to see her," Steve slurs, pointing past Lennox until he realizes he's aimed his finger at me. He blinks several times. "This is none of your business, Chelsea."

"It's going to be a cop's business." I stop beside Lennox. "Whichever one who comes to arrest your drunk ass if you don't leave right now."

"I'm not doing anything wrong." Steve takes a step across the threshold, but Lennox blocks him, and I close the gap he might try to slither through. His eyes finally focus on mine. "I need to talk to her."

"She doesn't want to talk to you, man," Lennox says.

Steve puffs his chest out and takes another step in, pushing against Lennox.

"Hey!" Lennox shouts, shaking his head as John joins us.

"You!" Steve shouts at John. Invigorated, he tries to push past Lennox to get to him.

"No. This isn't happening. Not here. Not tonight!" Lennox holds his arm out. Steve pushes against him.

John and I reach for him, ready to forcibly remove him, when a small voice comes from behind.

"What are you doing here, Steve?" Morgan stands a few feet back.

We look back at her.

Steve stops pushing. "You're not answering texts. You won't take calls. There's no other way to get to you—"

"She doesn't want you anymore!" I shout. "She wants you to stay the fuck away from her. What part of that don't you understand?"

"Let him in," Morgan says.

I swivel around, scowling. "What?"

"I'll hear him out," she says, focusing her stare on him. "I'll listen this one time, and that's it."

"You don't owe this asshole anything," John says.

"Move," Steve says, pushing past Lennox.

"Don't let him in!" I shout, holding my hands in front of me like a linebacker to block him, but Lennox steps aside.

Steve shoves past John, and Lennox has to hold John back. The sight sends goosebumps over my arms and panic fluttering through my chest. The same as that night.

Steve's careful not to touch me as he brushes by. He gives me a dangerous look. My skin crawls; there's an angry determination behind his eyes one wouldn't expect from someone who's as drunk as he must be, but I've seen it before.

It reads *don't fuck with me, or else.*

It says *how dare you try to stop me.*

It says *I win.*

I turn to Morgan, my heart in my throat. "If he stays, I go."

She avoids me altogether, choosing to look at the floor instead. She won't choose me. She'd rather expose herself to whatever gaslighting, toxic harassment he has in store for her today.

I won't be a part of this. I hold to my word. I grab my coat off the hanger and shoot Ellie an apologetic glance. I step toward the door. Lennox gently grabs my arm but I pull away.

"I can't," I mutter to him. We exchange a look, and for a moment, I know he sees me. All of me. The pain in my eyes, the betrayal of my friend, the loss of control, and the indignant fire that burns inside as another drunk abuser gets what he wants—another stroke in the win column.

Please, Lennox mouths to me, *stay.*

I turn back to Morgan, who still won't meet my eyes. If she asks me to, I will. If she asks me not to leave her alone with Steve, I'll stay by her side, like always.

She finally looks from me to Steve. Although there's skepticism in her eyes, there's a curiosity there, too. She walks toward Ellie, and the hallway beyond. She's going to talk to him alone. After everything he's done, she's giving him exactly what he wants. He follows her out of sight, down the hallway.

I shake my head and stride out the door, pulling my jacket on as the cool night air envelops me. I can't look at anyone. I can't see anything through a blur of tears. I want someone to come after me, but more than that, I need them to stay. I need them to protect her, because I can't anymore.

Doesn't she have a breaking point?

I hit mine when I was fourteen and my dad abused me in front of all my friends at my sleepover birthday party. He wasn't supposed to come home. Jordan agreed to supervise. He came in just after midnight, drunk, with a strange woman just as drunk as him. They started making out in front of all of us like we weren't even there. He smacked her butt as she went upstairs, then turned on the top step, and told my friends to get out. I told him he was being unfair. That they couldn't just leave. They had no way to get home.

He came back down and asked me if I was back-talking him. Before I could answer, he grabbed me by my hair and dragged me up to my bedroom. The girls shrieked as I screamed for him to let go. He beat me, leaving me slumped in the corner. My girlfriends came to be with me until one by one, their parents came to get them.

They weren't allowed back.

We never spoke about what happened, but the rumours did a lap around school about it. Jordan and I were the kids whose dad was an abusive alcoholic. They never caught him. Never took us away from him. A thorough beating was always just around the corner, and it didn't take much to set him off.

Just like Steve. They're playing with fire, letting him in —letting him be alone with her.

I stalk toward the beach, stopping as my feet hit the sand. I haven't set foot here since Austin. I head left, away from our bonfire spot, away from the direction we carried him, and walk all the way to the water. I stop short of it as my boots sink in the sand.

The water rolls in, almost touching my boots and out again, over and over. I let myself cry. At first, it's in frustration, then sadness, and then frustration again. I'm helpless. You can't help someone who doesn't want to be helped, but can't Morgan see she's made a mistake? It'll never be over for Steve until he's finished with her.

The reflected light of the moon shines a path across the water toward our bonfire spot down the beach, as if showing me the way to the place I belong. But I'm stuck. I can't go back. Not to the house. Not to the bonfire. I shiver as the waves roll back and forth, wondering if Steve's gone by now. If he started getting out of hand, they'd have stepped in. They'd throw him out, between John and Lennox, they could do it. It only took one man last time. I might be able to hear the shouting from here, if there was any.

I walk back to the road and a woman in a puffy vest walks by with a small, white dog. She nods to me with a smile, and I nod back, going through the motions as hope fills me that he's finally gone. Maybe we can deal with our problems together tonight. What other choice do we have?

I squint toward the house as I cross the road. I don't see Steve's car.

A couple passes me on the other side of the street, walking toward the beach. I stare after them, wondering if they'll be the people to find him. How many people have walked by Austin's body?

Maybe Steve's gone. My boots thump against the wooden front porch and I stop at the door. Should I knock? I should be able to just walk in, but I left. I abandoned them. Now I'm coming back. I take a deep breath and twist the knob.

They'll be happy to see me come back. I know Lennox will, at least.

The thought calms me enough to step inside and hang my jacket on the hook. The house is dark and quiet. Maybe they had to drag Steve out. Maybe Morgan's upset.

The dining room is just as we left it. Candlewax pools at the base of the holders, with only one three-wick left flickering in the middle of the table, and the remnants of our meals cool on our plates.

An uneasy feeling stirs inside as the silence lingers. Maybe they all fought over what to do about Austin...

I step into the dark living room, expecting to see them all sitting there, but it's just Lennox on the couch. His head is tilted—staring ahead at the bay window. That's strange...

"Hey," I barely let out the word as his blood-soaked shirt comes into view. "What—" I gasp.

What happened, I ask myself over and over. I follow the blood up his chest, to the gash in his neck where the blood still trickles.

I stumble back toward the hallway, trying to catch my breath, clutching my chest.

"Lennox," I whimper.

Something moves in the shadows of the dim hallway. There's something there. Someone. I take a slow step forward, my whole body shaking. As I reach out for the light switch, I notice something lying on the floor of the hallway further down. Ellie, on her back, nearly where I last saw her. Where I left her.

I take a step toward her. Blood pools on the hardwood beneath her, and a circular blot of red stains her floral blouse. She was stabbed.

I hesitate to reach for the light switch. I can't turn it on. Someone has a knife, and they could still be here. I can't call attention to us.

"Ugh-ha," Ellie's gasp comes from behind me, and I jump, clutching my sweater against my chest as her hand rises from her side, dripping red.

"Ellie." I drop to her side. My shaky knees are warm with blood. I grab her wet, sticky hand. "What happened?"

Her wide eyes stare into mine with pain and fear—she squeezes my hand, pulling me toward her. I lean in close to her face.

She lets out the words like a hiss. "Where's Lennox?"

I unintentionally shoot a quick glance toward the living room and my stomach churns. I can't tell her. I can't even form the words.

He's dead.

I open my mouth, but I start to heave, and she shakes her head, her eyes opening wide.

My blood runs cold as I freeze.

Is he behind me?

I turn over my shoulder, but I can't see through the darkness.

Steve's still here. I know it.

I turn back to Ellie and she pulls me closer by my hand. She's trying to warn me. Goosebumps cover my arms.

I lean in close to her lips.

"I told him what—what we did was wrong. Chelsea... I told him... eee..." She gasps and gurgles, squeezing my hand. "Eee said... we're all going to pay."

She's not making any sense. She's dying. I can't sit here and let her die.

"Hold on," I whisper, squeezing her hand before letting go and pulling my phone from my jeans pocket. I tap in 9-1-1, leaving bloody prints on my screen, and press it to my ear as I stand. I turn around in a circle as the phone rings, making sure he isn't behind me, creeping up on me from the shadows, waiting for his chance.

Morgan. What did he do to her? And John?

I take a step toward the bedroom and Ellie reaches for me. She doesn't want me to go—but if Morgan's alive...

I enter the back bedroom and a cold draft makes me shiver. Morgan and John's bodies lie on the floor at the end of the bed.

Blood soaks the front of John's shirt and spills from his neck, just like Lennox.

Lennox. I grab my stomach and keep the phone pressed to my ear, whispering the address to the dispatcher.

"Three-oh-six, Waterfront Road."

Lennox gave me the address a year ago, the night we met.

I take a shaky step toward Morgan, scanning the room for Steve.

A wet rattling fills the air. After another step, I place it. Morgan's still alive.

"Morgan." A tingling sensation washes over me as I drop to my knees. Blood spills from the side of her mouth. Her chest wound matches Ellie's, but her hands are folded over it, like they've been placed there. Like she's been manipulated for repose.

"Morgan," I whisper, an eerie chill washing over me. "I'm so sorry I left you. Help is coming." I grab her hand and as I squeeze, her eyes drift to the ceiling and her body shakes. "No. No."

She twitches for a few seconds as the dispatcher calls my name, but it echoes somewhere in the distance as the light fades from Morgan's eyes and everything goes still.

"No," I gasp, my breath caught in my throat as the phone slips from my hand onto the floor between us. I grab her arms and shake her gently. "Morgan, no. They're on the way. Please, stay with me. I love you."

I left her.

"Stay with me. I love you," I repeat over and over, asking of her what I couldn't give.

What I was too stubborn and scared and selfish to give.

The cold draft washes over me again, shocking me back into focus, like a warning to be vigilant. If Steve's still here, this isn't over. I grab my phone and stand, walking back into the hallway, toward Ellie. She's the only one left.

I press the phone to my ear. "We need an ambulance," I hiss. "*Now*."

"It's on the way," dispatch tells me.

"I think he's still here," I whisper.

"Who?" she asks.

"Steve," my voice shakes as I say his name. Not a whisper. Not a cry. Venomous.

I drop to Ellie's side and lean against the wall, using it to support us as I pull her close. She's still breathing, struggling.

"Stay with me," I tell her. "Please, you have to fight."

She turns her head toward me and her eyes seem to surrender as she releases a shaky breath without drawing in another. The hallway is silent. I hold my departed friend in my arms. A small voice is on the phone. It's fallen away from my ear again, casting its light flecked with a crimson coating into the hall.

What happened?

I can't breathe.

Boots thud into the hallway, across the hardwood floor. Heavy footsteps. Steve stands in the doorway of the back bedroom, his hands bloody, knife in his fist. Where did he come from?

He stares down at me, blood dripping off the blade.

I struggle beneath Ellie's body to stand, but the blood is slippery, and I can't get the traction with my feet. I can't catch my breath. I use my hands, keeping my eyes on him as Ellie's body slumps off of me and hits the floor with a *thunk*. My stomach churns as I use the wall to stand, gasping for air.

He steps toward me with inexorable patience, his heavy boot steps filling my ears.

Sirens wail in the distance and he stops, hesitating for a moment. Our eyes connect. Light from the lingering candle in the dining room glints off the sharp knife. The last thing my friends saw were those dead, dark eyes as he pierced their flesh with that knife.

He cut the life out of them.

He killed them all.

"What did you do?" I scream. I want to kill him. I want to kill him myself for what he did. I know he'll kill me too if he gets the chance.

The sirens wail another warning, knocking me back into focus. *Get out.*

Steve charges toward me, his boots slamming against the hardwood with a sucking release on the floor, sticky from blood.

I reach the front door first, my hand outstretched, grasping the knob, twisting it, but my bloody hands slip over the metal. I squeeze my eyes tight, ready for his fist to close with some part of me in his grip—for the knife to lance into me. I hear a muffled bang and glance over my shoulder. He pushes himself off the wall. He's stumbled.

I twist the knob again and fling the door open, lunging outside as I open my eyes.

"Chelsea!" Steve hollers from close behind.

Police cars screech to a halt on the other side of the white picket fence. I hold my bloody hands up and the horrible sound of his boots behind me resumes.

"Help," I scream. "He's going to kill me!"

"Get down," an officer shouts as he slides out of his car and draws his gun.

I drop to the path and two gunshots wrench the night. I can hear nothing else from the ringing in my ears, but I can picture it clearly; he drops to the floor, the last one to die.

I didn't think they'd stop him. I thought I was going to die.

They're all dead.

The thought hits me like I've been submerged in freezing water; painful, unbearable, inescapable.

"Officer, drop your weapon!" a deep, muffled voice shouts across the yard.

I raise my head as red light flashes across the white picket fence before me.

"They're all dead," I shriek, as two officers approach, guns drawn.

I scream into the night, despair ripping through me as the realization comes crashing down on me.

I left them, and now, they're all dead.

I'm alone.

25

A fter I finish bringing the last of my boxes into the basement, I lean against the floral wallpaper in the hallway. The frosted glass on both sides of the front door allow a small amount of light from the gray afternoon in. I stare at the door as the light fades. Molly will never walk through it again, and Jordan, Bella, and Timmy will return to a house with no mom and no wife.

No mom and no wife. That was the shape of our family. Our mom passed after battling cancer. Dad wasn't an alcoholic until after mom passed. Cirrhosis caught him a decade ago. I can't bear the thought of the cycle repeating itself.

Jordan wouldn't do that. He wouldn't let Bella and Timmy go through what we did.

Our dad probably hadn't planned on becoming an alcoholic, either. It was the grief after a loss. My therapist once said that grief is just the extra love we never got to express. It was too much for my father to bear sober.

Jordan's never loved anyone more than Molly—except the kids. When they come here, they'll be faced with the empty space Molly used to fill. I have to be here for them. I have to make sure that doesn't happen, but I can't do what my brother asked and bring Bella home if she'll be in danger. I pull the envelope from my jeans pocket and read it again.

THEY PAID for what they did. Now it's your turn.
Tell me the truth, Chelsea, or more will pay.
The house. Waterfront Road. Midnight.

I READ it to Kellan over the phone as soon as I got it, and she said she'd come over after school so we can work through my options. I fold the letter and tuck it back in my pocket.

Passing the front door, I step into the small living room. I pace before the front window as the sky's last champagne streaks fade. I check the driveway each time it comes in sight, counting the minutes since school's been out.

Kellan's black car drives down the street toward the house and I rush to the window.

No—not Kellan's car. That's Cam. What's he doing here?

He parks on the road in front of the boulevard and gets out as the streetlights flick on. As he strides up the driveway, past my car, he takes a look inside.

"What are you doing here?" I whisper, peeking out

the front window and taking a step back so he can't see me.

Is he here to see Jordan again? For what?

He wasn't shocked to see my car. It didn't even phase him. How could he have known I was here? This is the last place he'd look.

I meet him at the front door as he knocks, every thought of avoiding the pain of confrontation overridden by curiousity. I open it and he strides in, not missing a beat. I step aside so he doesn't bump into me.

"Cam? What's going on?"

He gives me a cold look. "Were you expecting someone? You were right by the door."

"Kellan's coming over soon. Why?"

He turns back to me with a stoic look. "You're not answering my calls."

"I've been busy, Cam, and it's been hard—"

He rests his hands on his hips. "Callie told me you came by the house today."

I nod. "I came to get some of my things."

"You didn't try to see me." He's almost indignant.

Why is he being like this?

I close the door over and turn back to him. "How did you know I was here?"

He looks around and when he spots the living room, he walks in. He never just barges in anywhere. This is so strange.

I follow him. "Cam, you're scaring me. I'm sorry for everything, okay? I should have come to you sooner about how I was feeling."

"How long?" he asks with pain in his eyes. "How long have you known you didn't want to be with me?"

I didn't know—not really—until the blackmail letter came. In my heart, I've known I'm not good enough for him for most of our relationship. We met at the local café a few months after the night my friends were murdered. I couldn't believe I was even interested in someone at the time, but he was so kind, and patient, and the distraction felt... not good, but more complete, with all I was missing.

Now, I feel like I'm standing across the room from a stranger.

I stop on the other side of the living room's coffee table from where he stands, trying to decide on an answer that won't upset him more. "I shouldn't have said yes when you proposed."

He shakes his head. "This isn't like you. What's going on with you? I know you're hiding something from me."

I crane my neck back. "Cam, I know *you* lied *to me*."

He stares, frowning, shaking his head, but he doesn't speak.

"Why are you here?" I ask. "How did you know I was here?"

Has he been following me?

"What did I lie about?" he asks.

I rest my hands on my hips and look around the living room that he so easily marched into, like he's been here before. Because he has. "Cam, don't play dumb."

He presses his lips together and his eyes look up to the right, like he's evaluating whether he should confess that he's been here before to see my brother.

"Why did you do it?" I ask.

His expression changes, his face contorts as he squints at me. "You think you're the only one who knows how to use people?"

"Use people—" I echo the sentiment his sister shared with me. "You—used my brother? For what?"

He frowns, shaking his head. "Your brother?"

"I know you were here to see him the other day."

He rubs his hand over his mouth, shaking his head. "Jordan told me—"

"Yeah, fine, I did." He clenches his jaw.

"Cam, why did you just say you used my brother? And why did you lie about it?"

His nostrils flare as he stares with contempt, the living room almost void of light.

"Cam? Answer me."

He rubs his chin and shakes his head, walking toward the front door. "I'm not doing this."

"Not doing what?" I ask as he walks by.

He stops and looks back. "You know I was trying to get you the support you needed. I always tried, but it never made a difference."

I FREEZE, blinking at him. "Cam, why did you come here? How did you know I was here? Have you been following me?"

My cell phone vibrates at my side as he shakes his head and strides to the door.

"I said I'm not doing this," he says. "I've tried with you, and if you're done with me, then fine."

I follow him to the door as he opens it. "I know you tried to help me. I'm sorry. This isn't your fault. I never meant to hurt you."

"You've known for months now that you didn't want to be with me, but you waited until now to tell me? That look." He nods to me. "That's the one I'm used to from you. It's the look you give when you're keeping something from me. When you're *lying*. I wanted you to tell me what's going on, but you won't."

"You followed me. Didn't you?"

"I love you." His chest heaves as he holds the door open. "I thought I'd try with you, one last time. Give you one chance to tell me the truth. I should have expected this."

He leaves me in the doorway and I watch him stalk down the driveway to his car.

My cell phone vibrates by my side again.

Jordan: *We're being transferred to the children's hospital tonight. Could you come before 8 to pick up some of the kids' things?*

Jordan: *Could you also bring the file folder in my office cabinet labeled Health, Home, Auto, and Life Insurance please? Bottom drawer of the desk.*

I look up from my phone as Cam drives off, and step back inside, out of the early evening chill, closing the door behind me. I jog upstairs to the office and tap Kellan's name on my cellphone. I have to let her know I'll be late. She should have been here by now, too.

"Hello, Chels?" she says.

"Hey, where are you right now?"

"I'm sorry, I'm still at the school—"

"That's okay. I have to go to the hospital and bring my brother some things first." I open the filing cabinet and scan through the folders.

"That's okay. I'm going to be here for a little longer. Chels, I found out where Austin's parents live. A coach friend of mine from another school had him on the football team. I looked up his alumni information, and I'm looking into it more now, but I think maybe I should go and see them."

"What? No."

"I'll tell them I used to be friends with Austin a long time ago, and I was wondering if they knew where he was."

I grab the folder and close the cabinet with my hip, running it back downstairs. "Kellan, this is risky. I don't want you involved in this on that level."

"The blackmailer wants to meet you at midnight. If we can find out who they are before then, we have some power."

I know she's right. It's our only shot, but it doesn't make it easier. "I should be there with you. Can you wait?"

"We don't really have time, and you have to go to the hospital. Chelsea, I was thinking. Is there someone new in your life? Someone you met recently?"

"No, not that I can think of..."

"What about Oz?"

"Well, he's not really new. We've known him for a year, now."

"I just can't help but wonder what triggered the black-mail letter. Try to think about anything you might have said to someone, even accidentally."

"I wouldn't have shared anything about that night, Kellan. I talked to Oz about the memorial, but that was it." I stop by the front door, gripping the folder. "I appreciate it you doing this. Keep in touch. Let me know what you find out, and we'll meet after, okay?"

"Okay."

"Kellan." I can't hide the fear and desperation in my voice, and I don't want to. She knows what happened to my family. I need her to stay vigilant. "Be careful."

"I will."

26

An odd feeling remains with me as I walk down the hospital hallway, approaching the kids' room. I press my cool hands against my warm cheeks and take a deep breath before entering. Jordan stands from his chair between the beds, and as I approach, he doesn't smile. I hand him the file folder.

"Aunt Chelsea," Bella whispers, pointing to Timmy, asleep on the bed. "Mister Camel."

He has the stuffed camel tucked under his arm and Bella holds her lion up, giving it a big hug.

"I'm so glad you like them," I whisper, giving her a wide smile before turning back to my brother.

"The kids wanted to see you," he says with a half-hearted smile. The way the last words hang, I can tell he has more to say. Something heavier.

"What is it?" I ask.

He waves me toward the door and I follow him. He looks over his shoulder and lowers his voice. "The detective looking into the crash came to see me."

I lean in closer. "What did they say?"

"He canvassed the houses of the people who live on the concession we were driving on. One of the homeowners said he was out raking leaves and saw a black car speed by around the time of the accident, going the opposite direction of where Molly's parents live." A black car. That's something. "He didn't get the plate. He had no reason to. Doesn't remember the make, either, but he said it was someone in a bright blue baseball cap driving."

I remember Cam in the kitchen, during our breakup, wearing his blue baseball hat.

"Okay," I huff. "Can they do anything with that?"

"No, but his next move is to check with the houses on that street, in that direction, and see if any of them have security cameras that would cover the road the driver was on. It's not much, but it could lead us to video. They could get the plates and question the driver. Chels... we might really find who did this."

He grabs me, pulling me in for a hug, and squeezes me tightly.

"That's great," I whisper.

"I just want to know," he says near my ear, choking on his words, "why? Why did this happen?"

Because of me.

I didn't do it, but this is my fault. The blackmailer is after me. I struggle with the thought, unable to push it away as Jordan holds me close. If he finds out Molly's death is my fault, he'll never forgive me, regardless of what he thinks I did or didn't do.

He pulls away and squeezes my arm, wiping the tears from his eyes. "I'm just so glad you're here, Chels."

The lump in my throat grows so big I can't speak.

He takes a few steps back into the room and I follow. Bella sits on the end of Timmy's bed, each with their new stuffed toys in hand.

What if the blackmailer is Cam? It doesn't make any sense, but... neither did his visit. The thought eats at my stomach, leaving a heavy, cold feeling of guilt in its wake. It's more than a thought. It's a feeling.

"Jordan, you know when Cam came to see you?"

He nods.

"Was there anything else he said? Anything he asked you that you can remember?"

He turns back to me and bites his lip, thinking. I wait for his answer, but he walks past me again toward the door. I follow, and he stops before the hallway, but keeps his back turned to me.

"I didn't want to get into it with everything going on— but there's been something I've been thinking about since Cam came to see me the other day."

Dread grows in the pit of my stomach as I wait for him to continue.

"He asked me why I stopped talking to you, and I told him I just couldn't understand why Steve would have... done what he did. When the police questioned me, I told them how Steve and I hung out that day, and he seemed so normal, or his new normal after the breakup. He was trying to convince me to go to this party in the city. I told him I didn't want to be the third wheel." He turns to me. "He was seeing someone new, y'know? Did you know that?"

I shake my head, no. I want to ask why it matters. I want to tell him it didn't stop him from trying to get Morgan back, but he continues.

"Sure, Steve still had feelings for Morgan. I didn't deny that to the police. He still talked about her. But he was moving on. There's no way he did it, Chels. Steve was a lot of things to a lot of people, but he wasn't a murderer." He shrugs and shakes his head. "And I told Cam that. I told him you and I would never see eye to eye on it. You know what he said? He asked me why I take it out on you."

Cam was always trying to help. He was trying to defend my position and get the support he knew I needed. I swallow at the lump in my throat, but it won't go away.

"I don't know why I took it out on you, because I know you didn't do anything wrong. Instead of being grateful you weren't killed, I just had to be right about something you experienced in a totally different way. I'll never understand what you went through, and... I believe you, okay? I've thought about it, and I think you were just trying to save yourself. You must have really thought he was going to kill you—but Chelsea—I don't think he would've. I'm not mad at you anymore. I don't want to waste time trying to be right, and I'm sorry I've left you to deal with it on your own all this time. Do you know how it feels to have you here, after I did that to you?"

I touch his arm and he flinches at the unexpected gesture. "Don't think about it, okay? Do you know how thankful I am to be with you again, and the kids? There's nothing—" I say through tears, "nothing I want more than to be here for you."

He nods, his hand covering mine. "Can we just agree to leave it in the past?"

I nod as my cell phone vibrates in my pocket. I check the notification. Kellan, with an attachment.

Jordan steps to the side and hoists a bag full of items, handing it to me. "Thanks for taking this home for us. When you come visit us, we might need some other things, too."

"Of course." I take the bag. "No problem. Jordan?"

He stares at me the way he used to, a benevolent look that always made me feel proud.

"I'm sorry this is happening." I squeeze his arm and step past him, out into the hallway.

I take out my cell phone. A new message notification comes up from Kellan.

"Chels," Jordan says as I walk down the hallway. I look back. "There was one other thing Cam said that was a little odd."

I stop. The bad feeling in my gut returns.

"He asked if you knew someone named Austin. I think that's the name. I told him I didn't remember and asked who that was. He said he thought it was an old friend of yours."

My heart pounds in my ears as I struggle to breathe. "Austin?"

He nods and shrugs.

Cam knows who Austin is.

"Chels?" Jordan lifts his head, nodding to me. "Call me, okay? I love you."

I stop, swallowing at the lump in my throat. "I love you, too."

And I'm sorry.

As he steps back into the room, I catch the glossy shine on his eyes in the fluorescent light of the hallway.

My phone vibrates in my hand, ringing this time, and I tap the green button by Kellan's name.

"Did you see it?" she asks, an urgency to her tone.

"What? What is it?"

"Look."

I pull the phone from my face and tap the text. A photo appears.

Four teens in football uniforms. Their arms wrapped around each other.

John, Murray, Austin, and Cam.

"Chelsea?" Kellan's voice calls to me.

I press it back to my ear, my hand shaking, my legs weak beneath me.

"Did you see?" she asks.

"It's Cam," I sputter, my body cold as my thoughts catch up to my instincts. "Cam's the blackmailer."

"Come over, okay?" she asks, but I can barely hear with my heart pounding in my ears. "Come to my place, now."

The video footage we watched of Cam's mailbox. That's why we never saw anyone else leave the letter.

The black car, blue baseball hat.

He killed Molly.

He ran my family off the road.

I can't breathe.

"Chelsea?"

As it all falls together, I'm falling apart.

I need her. I need help.

"I'm on my way."

27

I can't bring myself to put the key in the ignition. I sit clutching my keychain, listening to the echoes of screeching car wheels, and people talking as they walk behind my car.

All the answers I was looking for unfolded before me after what Jordan told me and the picture Kellan sent, but it's like I can't accept it. I can't believe Cam, the man I was engaged to, the man I lived with, slept with every night, could do this to me.

You think you're the only one smart enough to know how to use people?

That's what he said when I called him out on his lie.

How is it possible? How could he have been using me to—to get the truth about Austin?

And why?

Without thinking, I pick up the phone and tap his name, putting the call on speaker.

"Chelsea?" The hum of traffic surrounding him buzzes in the background.

His voice gives me chills. I grab the steering wheel and lean in toward the speaker.

"Cam? What have you done?"

Breathing follows, drawing out the tension, and I can't take it.

"You've been blackmailing me," I say, holding my breath as I wait for his response.

I need it to not be true. There has to be another explanation.

Only breathing follows again.

"Cam?"

"I never expected to have feelings for you when I found you at the coffee shop—followed you there, really. I wanted answers—I knew you had them."

"What are you talking about? You followed me to the café that day we met? Why?"

But I know. The truth is inescapable now.

"Austin Cann was my best friend."

He knew we were connected, somehow. Was he the friend Ellie warned me about? Was he the one who came to see them?

My heart races as I try to figure out my next move. "Cam—"

"You owe Austin's family the truth. You owe his memory the truth." A pause follows, traffic filling the silence. "You know what hurts the most? Everybody wrote him off. Nobody's looking for him. When you live a life like he did, spontaneous, travelling, no responsibilities, no attachments...That's what you all counted on, wasn't it? That no one would think it was weird to not hear from him for a while. Didn't hurt that he was depressed after Murray died and everybody knew it.

That's one thing I don't get, Chelsea, is how John could have been part of it. He lost his brother. Austin was a brother to him, like he was to me. Austin wasn't always around—he had his own demons—but when he was, he was a damn good friend."

It's like John's words are echoing back to me. It's exactly what John thought before he discovered the truth.

Cam must not know about Austin's involvement in Murray's death.

I shouldn't have called him. I need time to think. I need to get to Kellan.

I start the car and reverse out of my spot as he speaks again.

"When we first met, I planned on becoming your friend. Confronting you in an honest way wasn't going to work. I tried that already. I knew it would take a long time. After the first few months of knowing you, I couldn't believe you'd have been involved in his disappearance. Maybe it was because I was falling for you. That's what I tell myself now."

As I pull out of the parking lot, beneath the navy blue night sky, I remember the letter in my pocket. He came to Jordan's to give me one last chance to confess. What did he plan for tonight, at midnight? His last resort? His final revenge?

"I knew something was up when Austin didn't answer my text for three weeks," he says. "Austin never went that long without responding to me. I bet he didn't for John, either. Something you all didn't count on? The location setting on his phone was always on. I made sure of that after Murray passed. Austin was devastated, depressed, and withdrawing from all of us. I wanted to be able to find him... in case. He sent me a text saying he's off to his next big adventure, and then his location vanished. You know where it was? His last known location? The waterfront."

He wasn't the one who filmed the video. Someone sent it to him. It began at the waterfront for him. He wants it to end there, too.

"I went, looking for any sign of Austin. I was terrified he drowned himself. I went every day and night for the few hours I could spare between work and I showed his picture to anyone I could find. I did that for a month until someone recognized him. They said he was down at the water sometimes, at bonfires with a group of friends. I thought that was strange. Austin never told me about that. Never invited me. I wasn't sure if I should believe the guy at the beach, but he told me where one of the friends lived, right down the road. Three-oh-six, Waterfront Road. I had hope for the first time, and when I knocked on Lennox and Eliana's door, I thought I'd finally get the help I needed to find my friend."

It comes back to me, slowly. The night they all died, Ellie told me people came. A man, and a police officer. Cam's dad was an officer, then...

"You spoke to Lennox and Ellie? When?"

"That's what you ask me? After everything I told you, you just want to know what he said?" There's a pause and the traffic in the background dies down a little so I can hear his breathing. "Him and his sister. They were both there. I showed them Austin's picture and asked if they knew him. Lennox said no. Why would they lie about knowing him?"

But he knows. He has the video. He's trying to get me to admit it. Is he recording me?

"Same reason as you, Chelsea. You all know what happened to him."

All my muscles tense as I stop at an intersection.

"I asked my dad to go the next day and ask them if they knew him. I begged him. He said it would be a waste of time, and he seemed convinced they were telling the truth, because after that, he told me Austin was out living his wild bachelor life, and I should let him live it because I had my own responsibilities. Nobody wanted to listen to me. Nobody, until Eliana."

Was that why she was so desperate for us to tell the truth?

"I went the next day. Lennox was gone. I begged her to talk to me. I told her I didn't want to bother her, and I wasn't sure why they lied, but that the man on the beach told me he'd seen you all together. I told her Austin was my best friend, that he'd do anything for me if I asked, and I had to do this for him. You know what she did?"

I close my eyes, imagining him confronting Ellie, all alone. The fear she must have felt. The guilt—the shame I know so well.

A car honks behind me, and I jump, staring at the green light ahead. I press the gas pedal, clutching the wheel.

"She cried. Eliana cried on my shoulder and told me she was so sorry, but she couldn't help me. I cried, too, because I knew in that moment, the worst *had* happened. I knew she had something to do with it. Why else would Lennox have flat-out lied about knowing him? You know what else I knew? That I wouldn't stop until I found him, no matter what it took."

He couldn't have taken the video. Someone sent it to him. It must have been Steven.

"What I didn't know," he says, a new depth to his voice. "Was that it would take getting close to one of the people who killed him, trusting you with my whole heart, and letting go of my search. I didn't know that quitting Austin and putting my full trust in you would get me close enough to the truth, but it has, Chelsea. You're going to tell me the truth. I'm going to make you."

28

This whole time, I kept secrets from him, and he did the same to me.

Secrets are one thing, but to put my family in danger —kill my sister-in-law—all to find the truth about Austin? This isn't Cam. It can't be.

"Cam," I say, my voice shaking. "We've been together for five years. We had a life together... How can you do this to me? How can you try to hurt me—the people I love?"

"I thought I knew you, but I didn't, and I didn't know you were involved, but after that night—after they all died—you were the last one standing. I had to talk to you. I knew confronting you would get me the same results as it did your other friends, so I tried a different approach with you. The long game. I had no idea it would take this long, and that you would take up a place in my life where I actually cared about you—loved you. That it would become less about making you feel safe enough to tell me the truth, and more about making you feel safe in life, because despite all your faults, I thought you deserved that. I thought you deserved peace. That maybe you didn't know Austin, or what happened."

But now that he knows, he'll do whatever it takes to get revenge? He'll try to kill my family? All the love he talks about—it isn't real. He's trying to trap me. That's what this is.

"I saw it," he says, pausing. There's silence in the background. "I saw the picture. You saved it to my computer, Chelsea." The group of us around the fire with Austin. "That's when I knew I had to do something. I gave you the opportunity to come clean about Austin."

He knew he had to do something... He found the person with the video footage of that night, or they found him. Maybe it was on Steven's phone from that night? But how could he have gotten that?

"You are guilty. That's why you suffer, Chelsea. That's why you were about to confess. It's your conscience. You underperform at everything in life because you don't feel like you deserve good things. My theory is because you don't really have to try very hard in life. Everyone handles you with kid gloves, including me. I knew I was enabling you. I catered to you, and you never compromised for me. You let me take care of you, but you never truly let me in. In hindsight, I bet you're glad about that, but it's not a life, Chelsea. Admit what you did to Austin."

"Or what, Cam? What are you going to do?"

A long silence lingers in my car as I imagine what he had planned for me tonight. What horrific pain he's ready to put me through—worse than anything I've experienced.

But it couldn't be.

I watched my friends die.

I held Morgan's hand as she choked to death on her own blood.

I held Ellie against my body as her life slipped from hers.

Ellie's last words echo in my mind as she held my hand, dying in that hallway.

I told him what—what we did was wrong. Chelsea... I told him... Eee said... we're all going to pay.

I thought she meant about Steven, and how Austin dragged him away that night, scaring him off. That Steven wanted revenge against all of us that night.

But she didn't say Steven's name. I thought that was because it was obvious. Was she trying to finish what she started to tell me before I left that night? That the man she spoke to came back? That she told Cam what we did was wrong, but he came back and told them they'd all pay?

The thought terrifies me as I turn onto the main road through Newcastle.

What if Cam went to the house on Waterfront when I was gone that night, confronted my friends, tried to get answers out of them about Austin? And when they wouldn't tell him...

"Were you there that night?" I ask.

"Which one, Chelsea?" He asks, his voice strong as a car door slams in the background. "The night your friends died or the night you all killed Austin? I've been waiting years for the truth. Their deaths didn't make me feel any better. I don't want to hurt you."

Panic fills my chest.

"If you want to make things right, there's still time. You know what you have to do," he says, and the call ends.

I press my fingers against the note in my pocket.

The house on Waterfront Road at midnight.

29

I race up the driveway past Kellan's car to the front porch, and rap my knuckles against her door. I step back, panting, and check my phone, though I know no one's called or messaged; I can't help the nervous habit. Almost ten. Two hours. I knock again. This time I stay close to the door, listening. No footsteps. No voices. Maybe she's out back.

It's too cold to be out here.

Rubbing my hands over my arms to keep warm, I walk around the side of the house. I follow the unlit string lights to the backyard. Her patio set sits empty. The leaves on the oak trees rustle in the wind, filling the midnight black backyard with a gentle hiss. I round the table to the sliding glass doors. On the other side of the glass, in the dark kitchen, a glass of red wine sits on the counter alongside a butcher block with some sort of diced vegetable. I take a step closer, and there's someone on the floor. Kellan.

I yank on the handle, stumbling with the force as it slides open.

"Kellan," I call to her.

Without the glare from the reflection on the glass, I can see her clearly, positioned on her back, hands over her chest. Her bloody chest. She's not moving.

Morgan. That's how I found Morgan.

Is she... no. Please, no.

I inch toward her, scanning the kitchen, and pull my cell phone from my pocket. As I reach her side, I notice the sneakers sticking out from the other side of the counter. Someone else is here, laying on the floor. I creep around.

It's Cam.

His body lies face down in a pool of blood on the white tile, his red hand clutching the metal handle of a kitchen knife.

"Holy shit," I whisper, pressing my hand to my mouth, my fingers trembling.

What happened?

I take a step back and dial 9-1-1 as a sharp gasp comes from behind me. I jump, turning as Kellan clutches at her chest, staring at me with wide eyes.

"Chelsea," she gasps.

She's alive. Relief washes over me.

"Hang on," I tell her, returning to her side and dropping to my knees. "I'm getting help."

I grab one of her bloody hands with one of mine and press the phone to my ear as a sick feeling sinks in my stomach. Déjà vu.

"I need an ambulance to... to Fifteen Fowler's Way. Two people are badly wounded. Stabbed." Pain courses through me with the word and I squeeze her hand harder.

"Ow," she hisses, yanking it away. Blood drips down the large gash along the inside of her forearm, and she stares at it, blinking. "I think I killed him."

"What was he doing here?"

He was headed here while we were talking. He knew what he was going to do.

She lifts her head off the floor and winces.

"Kellan, just stay still—"

"He wanted to know what I knew about Austin." She rests her head against the floor again. "He was questioning me. Trying to get it out of me. I didn't tell. I wouldn't break."

I notice the purple bruise forming beneath both her eyes.

"He tried to b—beat it out of you?" I cast a quick glance over my shoulder, but there's no movement from Cam.

"He tried to take me," she cries. "He grabbed me, and I had the knife. Oh, God, Chelsea, I killed him."

He was going to bring her to the house on Waterfront. He was going to make me tell the truth or else she'd die. He'd kill us anyway. Kill us both.

My hands tremble as I press my tongue to the roof of my mouth, trying to keep from swallowing it. You can't just swallow your tongue, but as I try to rationalize, my skin goes cold and clammy. I can feel my tongue slipping down my throat. I'm sure of it.

He said he'd do anything for the truth. This is beyond brutal. The blood on her chest is from her arm. The blood on our hands...

Kellan stares up at me, wide-eyed. "You're having a panic attack."

I freeze, sure my heart will stop at any moment if I dare move again. If I look away from the blood dripping down her arm. I can't breathe. The dispatcher tells me help is on the way.

The dispatcher's voice.

The stickiness of Kellan's blood on my hand.

The knife in Cam's hand.

It's all the same.

I gasp for breath, but I can't get a full one, staring down at Kellan as she grazes her fingers over the gash in her arm and presses her hand against it. The blood trickles out from between her fingers. I want to tell her it'll be okay, but I can't speak. I can't see straight. I'm going to die.

The phone slips from my hand to the floor by the counter, and Kellan's eyes open wide as she takes in the sight of me. Her eyes grow wider, still, until I turn and see Cam behind me. He struggles to his knees, reaching for the countertop for support. The knife is in his hand.

"Chelsea," Kellan hisses. "Oh, God, no." She gasps for breath. "Please. Don't let him—"

Cam pulls himself up, pointing the knife at us. Reality slips for me; the image of Steven, knife in hand, alternates between what I'm facing, from Cam's face, to Steven's, back to Cam's. It can't happen again. I can't let him kill us. Ellie's words echo in my mind as Cam stumbles toward us.

I told him what—what we did was wrong. Chelsea... I told him... eee said... we're all going to pay.

"You fucking bitch," Cam grunts, supporting himself with the countertop.

"Chelsea," Kellan gasps, shaking my hand.

I look down and notice the bloody knife with the wooden handle by her side.

Cam catches my eye, shuffling toward us. He's unsteady but determined. I don't recognize him anymore. He's not the man I knew.

Kellan hisses in pain and shoves my hand against the knife handle, but I can't stop staring at him.

Steven came at me with the knife. Without a word beyond my name. Because he didn't kill them. He was scared. He was trying to get out. He called my name. He was trying to tell me Cam killed them. I can't let it happen again.

I grab the knife and rise to my feet, my legs barely supporting me against the weight of my fear. "Why did you kill them?"

Cam stares down at Kellan, blood trickling from the corner of his mouth.

I hold the knife out, but it shakes in my hand. "You beat her, Cam? You fucking coward! You tried to get her to tell you about Austin, but she doesn't know—"

"She... knows... everything—" he starts, shoving his knife out before him.

Something heavy pushes against my side. Kellan presses her bloody hand against it to stand, grabs the knife from my hand, and lunges forward in one quick, practiced motion, plunging it into Cam's chest and out again. I gasp as his knife slips from his hand, clanging against the bloody tile. Kellan shuffles backward toward me, muffling her cries and cradling her bad arm against her chest.

I take the knife from her and stare at Cam in shock as she presses against her wound once more.

He drops to his knees, eyes wide.

Kellan sinks to the floor beside me, clutching her arm as she cries, "oh my God," over and over.

I couldn't protect them that night. I couldn't protect us tonight.

The panic swells inside my chest as I look down at her, "Kellan, I'm so sorry."

"He was going to kill us," she cries.

He came because I told him I was seeing Kellan. He asked if I was expecting someone, and I said her. I handed him a target on a silver platter.

"I'm so sorry." My body starts to shake. The adrenaline.

"He's crazy," she cries, looking up at me. "He wasn't going to stop."

"The police," I say, looking around for my phone. I realize I can breathe. I am keeping busy. I can breathe. "They'll be here soon."

I spot the phone just beneath the cabinet of the counter by the sink.

"Unlock the door for them," Kellan says, wincing, still on her knees, "will you, please? I'm—I'm losing a lot of blood."

I nod, taking shaky steps to the counter by the sink and grab a tea towel, bringing it back to her and wrapping it around her arm.

"Thank you," she whispers.

She's not mad at me—she doesn't blame me—but she should.

I rush down the hallway to the front door and twist the lock.

Where's Cam's car? Why didn't I see it when I came? It's in the driveway. I thought that was Kellan's. I thought that the other day at Jordan's, too. They look the same.

I turn back toward the kitchen, but the blue baseball hat hanging by the door stops me.

An eerie sensation sends prickling shivers across the back of my neck as I recognize Cam's hat and coat, hung below it. Why did he take off his coat?

I slip my hand in the pocket and hit his phone. Pulling it out, I glance over my shoulder toward the kitchen before tapping in Cam's password with trembling fingers. I open his messages and there are two most recent.

Unknown Number: *I'm worried about Chelsea.*

Unknown Number: *Call me and I'll tell you what I know.*

I shoulder-check again.

Cam said Kellan knew everything. What did he mean?

My mind races as I slip the phone back in his coat pocket and turn to the kitchen.

Kellan stands in the doorway, and I jump. "You okay?"

I nod. She shuffles back into the kitchen and I follow behind her.

She was so hurt before, she could barely move, but then when Cam started talking, she got up and stabbed him. She stopped him before he could say anything else.

Kellan stops a few feet away from Cam's body, staring at it, cradling her arm close to her chest.

Ellie's words echo back to me again.

"I told him what—what we did was wrong. Chelsea... I told him... eee..." She gasps and gurgles, squeezing my hand. *"Eee said... we're all going to pay."*

She was choking on her own blood. What if she didn't say *he*? What if she was trying to say *she*?

Kellan turns back to me, a bright red bloodstain growing on the cream tea towel. "What is it?"

I shake my head, staring down at my bloody knife. "I just can't believe he did it."

"No?" she asks. Her tone shifts. "You were quick to believe Steve did it. Why not Cam?"

My body goes cold like her stare as she studies me.

"I—I don't know," I stammer.

"He tried to kill me, Chelsea. Don't you see? I saved us." She slowly turns back to Cam.

I don't know how, and I don't know why, but I know Kellan killed my friends. I know she tried to kill my family. And now, Cam.

I grip the knife in my hand and approach her, slowly and carefully.

I have to be careful.

I need the truth.

30

Even though she's facing away from me ten feet across the kitchen, I know what comes next. She's going to kill me. My best friend's been the killer all along.

Somehow, she knows everything, just like Cam said. Cam, what were you caught up in? Was it just my lies, or hers, too? To get the truth out of her, I have to tell mine. That would have solved everything if we'd just done it that night when Austin died. If we'd just come clean with the truth. The truth isn't clean, though, and I'll never be. We can't hide anymore.

"I told you what I did, Kellan," I say, getting a better grip on the sticky wooden handle of my knife. "Now it's your turn."

She keeps her back to me, lowering herself to the ground. She's kneeling, but rises again, holding Cam's knife in her right hand—her good hand. She turns to me and I step to the side. If I'm right, she killed four of my friends with a knife like that, without any help. Now, five. I steal a glance at Cam's body. I'm out of my depth, but I don't need to beat her at what she does so well. I only need to hold out long enough for the truth.

The truth is what Cam wanted. That's what he meant when he referenced the note. The first one.

The video. The note in my pocket. They were from her. She's the only one that saw the first blackmail letter. She put that second note on my car windshield at the hospital because she knew I was going there. She's the one. She tried to kill my family.

"You tried to kill my brother and his family." I wait for a reaction, but her face remains stoic. "You killed his wife. You almost killed children!"

The look she provides, the one I thought meant she didn't understand or couldn't hide her feelings, has always been a mask. It's a front, like mine. Everyone in my life has been lying to me since that night, mirroring back what I've done to them.

"Why? Why did you go after my family?"

"It was pretty fun when you thought it was him." She tilts her head to the side, nodding behind her at Cam. "He wasn't trying to kill them. He was trying to get answers from your brother."

My heart aches for him as this new fact sinks in. I steal another glance at his body, hoping for movement. He never hurt my family. He didn't want to hurt me. He only wanted to find his friend and bring him justice. He died without discovering Austin's part in Murray's death. Maybe it's better that way—but did he have to die?

A hard lump forms in my throat as memories from our relationship flash before my eyes.

I actually started to care about you—love you... less about making you feel safe enough to tell me the truth, and more about making you feel safe in life, because despite all your faults, I thought you deserved that. I thought you deserved peace.

If you want to make things right, there's still time. You know what you have to do.

That's the last real thing he said to me. He was right.

Kellan lured him here. She's always so calm, so even-tempered, but it's never been about her. She's never been questioned about any of it. She's spent all these years living easy with what she's done.

"Why did you go after my family, Kellan?"

"You were going to the police. You told me you'd go to the house first, and then, you were going to confess before I knew who sent you that blackmail letter. I couldn't let that happen. I needed to know who else knew about that night. I went to Jordan's, and they were just leaving. I didn't have a plan. I just followed them out of their subdivision, onto some back roads, and as the night grew dark, and time ran out, I did what I had to do."

She rubs her fingers against the bloody, steel handle, then points the knife at me. I clench my stomach, remembering the delicate, precise force she just used to stab Cam. She was a champion fencer. She's going to do that to me, too. My heart races, my breath short. I have to keep focused.

"What happened that night, Kellan?"

"If I tell you, you know I'm going to have to kill you, right?" She smiles, taking the first step toward me.

I remain in place and say matter-of-factly, "You're going to try to kill me, anyway."

She releases a short huff and grins. "Finally catching on, Chels."

"Why did you kill my friends?"

"I was there that night." She takes another step closer. I want to retreat. Run for the door. But I'm not replaying history. This has to have a different ending. I keep freezing in the moments I need to act. I take a step closer to her and she stops, surprised, her brow twitching before she continues. "The night John killed Austin. Did you like my camera work? Pretty good, huh? Not as good as my editing, though. That was more recent, when I realized I needed to stop you from turning yourself in."

"You were there that night? How? Why?"

"I saw how you all treated Steve. Like some animal, less than human. You thought you were above it all."

I take another step closer, toward the counter. "You cared about Steve? You barely knew him."

She laughs again, and I wonder if she's registering that I'm advancing on her. "I bet you still think Morgan was the one who broke up with him. You're so naive. You'll believe whatever is convenient. Steve broke up with *her* to be with *me*."

I shake my head, no, but I believe her. She smiles again. It explains why Morgan never told me what happened that would make her finally end it. Jordan mentioned Steve moving on with someone else. But Steve never *really* moved on, and that's why. Breaking up with Morgan wasn't even his idea.

"You were jealous of her."

Kellan takes a quick step toward me and I take one back. "I wasn't jealous!"

I make note that when provoked she opens up and gets defensive. I'm too vulnerable to her. This is the price I pay, the true price for everything I've done. All my muscles grow tense as she continues, rivulets of blood pattering from her wrist to the floor, still.

"Steve was done with her. He couldn't bring himself to end it, so I gave him the courage he needed. Too bad he couldn't follow through when we got to the house. I should have seen it coming. I should have known his anger would dissipate by then. He was furious that night you all ran him off. That's why he agreed to make sure no one ever thought they could treat him like that again. I should have known he'd be too chickenshit to do what we'd talked about—never mind the things I planned as a surprise."

Images of my friends' bodies strewn about flash before my eyes, covered in blood, everything red.

"Kill them all?" I swallow the saliva pooling in my mouth as I glance down at her bloody knife. "Was that the plan?"

"Teach them a lesson," she says. She's proud, and when she's proud, she's still. "That's what Steve thought we were doing, anyway."

"But you knew the whole time you were going to kill them—at least Morgan. You wanted her out of the picture." Because she knew Steve regretted leaving her. She knew he was trying to get back with her. If she was there that night, she saw how jealous he was of John. I can't say it, though. I can't risk her coming closer. I need to buy a little more time.

"That really caught Steve off guard, when he let me in through the back window." The draft I felt. It was so cold. "I stabbed her as soon as I got in, and then John attacked me, and Steve protected me. Steve fought him off until I slit John's neck. The blood. You should have seen all the blood." She smiles and my stomach lurches. "Well, I guess you did."

"You killed them all? Just you?"

"Every single one," she laughs. "I thought you'd be there, too. Pity."

There's no real emotion in her voice as she admits she would have killed me, too. I'd have been collateral damage, at best. She was never really my friend—never really cared. Why couldn't I see it?

"When I finished, I tried to get Steve to leave with me, but he wouldn't leave her side. He folded her arms over her chest, like he was sorry, remorseful. It was pitiful." She shakes her head. "Did you like that touch when you saw me? Did it take you back?"

I gesture, no, but my body aches with rage. "So, you just left when you saw he chose *her*?"

"I didn't *just* leave." She scowls and takes another step toward me, less than three feet away, close enough to lunge with the knife. She could swipe at my neck like she did Lennox and John. Or will she stab me in the chest like Morgan, and Ellie, and Cam? "I wiped the handle of the knife off and handed it to Steve. Draped a towel over the windowsill and told him he had to come with me or take the fall. He chose right—at first." Her gaze drops for the first time.

That's why he wasn't in the room with me while Morgan died.

"What happened?" I ask, but I already know.

She's not looking at me anymore. It's as if she's back in that house, at the window, realizing after everything she did, he'd still choose Morgan. Her smile is gone. She's somber.

This was the heartbreak she told me about. The man who didn't choose her.

I take a small step back out of reach. My lower back touches the counter. I arrive at my destination. "He left you." She focuses on me again. "You crawled out the window, like the spineless psycho you are. He chose her. He'd rather be with a dead Morgan than a live monster like you."

My muscles tense as I wait for the attack I've provoked, but she remains still.

"I heard you scream." Her lips twist into a smirk. "After I left through the window, I didn't get far before your blood-curdling scream echoed through the neighbourhood. It sounded like raw pain, Chelsea, and I knew it was because of me. I did that." Her eyes light up. "I wonder if I can make you do it again."

Kellan darts in and jabs the knife at my chest, but I twist, and she misses, darting back where she was. She's so fast. She shakes her head at me, narrowing her gaze. "I'll make you a deal. You tell me where Austin's body is buried, and I'll make sure it's found along with Shay-Lynn's. Their families will know what happened to them. They won't have to wonder anymore."

My blood runs cold. "Shay-Lynn? That was *you*?"

She nods, pressing her arm against her chest, the tea towel fully soaked in blood. "Where's the body?"

"Tell me where Shay-Lynn is. What did you do with her?"

"She got a little too close to me, and unlike you, she paid attention. She knew I had secrets. She didn't know what they were, but she knew too much. Plus, after four years of thinking about what I'd done, I guess I developed a little taste for it. I set up fencing practice here one night. It was quite a matchup. She saw it coming, too, just like you did there." She waves the knife at me. "She just wasn't quick enough to beat me. I drove her car two cities over and took a midnight marathon, then buried her in the backyard, by the oak trees." She glances out the sliding doors for a moment, and I take a small step to the side, clutching my knife, wondering if it's time to fight back. Her reflexes are better, but if I can get her good arm...

She turns back to me and sighs. "I don't like cleaning up after my messes, and I'm in no condition to." She casts a quick glance at her bloody arm and looks back up at me with a confident smile. "I know what you're thinking, Chelsea. If you can work past your panic attacks for once and actually take a swing at me, kudos, but you better not miss. Now, where's Austin's body?"

Why does she want to know? She wants to pin it on Cam—pin it all on him. I have to keep her talking. I have to do what Cam said—what I know is right.

"He's buried close to the place we had our bonfires, between the tree line and the water, on the beach. I don't know exactly where. It was dark—"

A faint hint of sirens cry in the distance—the sound I've been waiting for.

"Not much time left," she huffs, squinting at me, scanning my body. "Now, where did Cam get you?"

She jabs at my chest again, predictably, and when I twist away along the counter's edge, she flips the knife in her hand and jams it into my stomach. I gasp as the impact takes my breath away, pressing back against the counter as she pushes the knife deeper, using her body weight.

I release a silent scream as the pain slices through me and Kellan smiles.

I'm stuck here. The pain is vicious, filling me without reprieve or remorse.

She pushes off me and I grasp at the knife in my stomach, slinking down against the cabinet.

"Don't worry, Chels." Her calm voice infuriates me as I hit the floor, the pain ripping through me again. "It hurts now, I know, but it won't for long. You want to know the best part? I've got it all set up so Cam takes the fall. For everything. For your friends, and Austin. Even Shay-Lynn."

The sirens wail grows louder as Kellan stands over me, staring in my eyes. For a moment, that siren is the sound of my pain and terror. I close my eyes and wait for the pain to end. Wait for my turn to die. Wait to see my family and friends again.

But I can't. I told the truth, and so did she, but I can't leave my family. If they'll have me, after all this, I'll be here for them. I have to be.

I summon the strength and breath I have left, like Morgan did, squeezing my hand. Like Ellie did, trying to tell me who killed them.

"Kellan," I gasp, opening my eyes wide as she reaches for the knife in my stomach.

She hesitates as car doors slam just outside. I grab her hand, wincing with the pain, squeezing it as shock fills her expression for the first time. She thought I'd try to stab her. She twists her lips into a grin, realizing I'm too weak, either physically or emotionally, but it doesn't match her eyes. It's the same sick smile my friends saw as she killed them, one by one. The same smile Shay-Lynn must have seen.

With the last of my breath, I turn my head to the left, and say, "look."

As the front door slams open, and officers call out through the house, Kellan's eyes drift to my cellphone beside my head, tucked just beneath the cabinet. The phone I'd called the police on. The call that's been connected the whole time, listening. Recording.

I draw in a final, shaky breath as she turns back to me, anger and defeat filling her fiery glare.

Officers surround us as it all goes dark, pulling her away from me. I drop my knife, losing control. My vision fades.

It's difficult to see things coming in the eye of a storm.

To learn the truth, I had to tell mine, and now it's all been recorded for the police to discover. If we'd told the truth the night Austin died, that would have stopped all the suffering. If we'd just come clean. No more hiding, Kellan.

I'm finally free.

Thank you for reading *I Heard You Scream*. If you enjoyed the story, don't miss Emerald O'Brien's latest psychological suspense releases...

We Don't Leave - a standalone domestic suspense novel
Who can you trust when you can't believe your own eyes?
The Waking Place - a standalone psychological suspense novel

Givers must set limits, for takers have none.

Follow Her Home - a standalone psychological thriller novel

She's desperate to leave the past behind her. But fear has a way of following.

What She Found - a standalone psychological suspense novel

It was supposed to be the perfect getaway, but a knock at the door could ruin their lives.

YOUR FREE EBOOK

Emerald would love to offer you a free ebook along with updates on her new releases.

Subscribe to her newsletter today on emeraldobrien.com

ACKNOWLEDGMENTS

Thank you to my beta readers, Kiersten Modglin, Meghan O'Flynn, and Shyla O'Brien. You helped me bring the story in my heart and mind to life on the page. I appreciate your encouragement, new ideas, understanding, and enthusiasm. Thank you for reflecting the story back to me with fresh eyes, your unique perspectives, and with such care that I'm so grateful to have received.

To Meghan O'Flynn, thank you for your integral developmental edits, and for guiding the way through the trees until I see the forest.

Thank you to K R Stanfield for your in-depth editing services and insightful feedback. I'm so grateful for your help.

Thank you to my colleagues in the book community for your support, encouragement, and sharing your knowledge with me. I'm proud to call you my friends.

For the continued support of my family and friends, I am forever grateful, and I love you all. Each and every person in my life who has supported me and my writing career hold a special place in my heart.

Thank you to my true-blue readers, review team, newsletter subscribers, and my reader group. Your company on this journey has been a pleasure.

ABOUT THE AUTHOR

Emerald O'Brien was born and raised just east of Toronto, Ontario. She graduated from her Television Broadcasting and Communications Media program at Mohawk College in Hamilton, Ontario.

As the author of unpredictable stories packed with suspense, Emerald enjoys connecting with her readers who are passionate about joining characters as they solve mysteries and take exciting adventures between the pages of great books.

I Heard You Scream is Emerald's 20th novel.

To find out more, visit Emerald on her website: emeraldobrien.com

If you enjoyed Emerald's work, please share your experience by leaving a review where you purchased the story.

Subscribe to her newsletter for a free ebook, exclusive content, and information about current and upcoming works.

ALSO BY EMERALD O'BRIEN

Don't miss these suspenseful and unpredictable reads by
Emerald O'Brien

Standalone Novels:

We Don't Leave

Follow Her Home

The Waking Place

What She Found

The Knox and Sheppard 5 Book Mystery Series:

The Girls Across the Bay (Book One)

Wrong Angle (Book One Point Five, free in Emerald's
newsletter)

The Secrets They Keep (Book Two)

The Lies You Told (Book Three)

The One Who Watches (Book Four)

The Sisters of Tall Pines (Book Five)

The Locke Industries Series:

The Assistant's Secret

The Nanny's Secret by best-selling author, Kiersten Modglin

Manufactured by Amazon.ca
Bolton, ON